Dedicated to Janet

CHAPTER
ONE

The gray-haired lady next to Charlie Callaway was reading from a copy of *Leslie's Illustrated Weekly*. Only later did he realize she was reading to him also.

"My goodness, listen to this, mister! In Kansas the women are trying to get the vote! Can you imagine that! Women wasn't put on this earth to vote! That's a man's business! A female's proper duties is to cook and clean house and have babies." She stared at him over iron-rimmed spectacles. "Isn't that right?"

Meekly Charlie nodded. "Yes, ma'am." She had been friendly — too friendly. At the moment he was wary of friendship with anyone.

"Tong wars in San Francisco!" She shuddered, showing him a lurid woodcut of a crowd of Chinamen running from a pig-tailed assassin who brandished a cleaver. "Oh, them bloody-minded Chinamen! I hear they eat rats, too!" Turning away, for which he was grateful, she stared out the window.

"Why, we've stopped! Now why is that? I do hope it don't make us late for Chambersburg! Do you know why we stopped, mister?"

Outside of Hanover Junction the cars of the Northern Central Railroad had come to a stop, clanging and banging in a stink of steam and hot oil. Charlie brushed soot from his stylish nankeen coat and leaned out the window. In the cinders beside the tracks a Union sentry with fixed bayonet was talking to the train crew. Because of the hiss of escaping steam and the rushing of the river below, Charlie could not catch the words. Quickly he drew back, closing the window; he did not care for the sight of blue uniforms.

"Nothing to be alarmed about, ma'am," he explained. "From the proximity of the river, I'd guess they're just taking on water. There's quite a grade ahead." To signal a desire for privacy, he took out his sweet potato — an ocarina — and began to play a small tune. But she was relentless; poking wisps of hair under her bonnet, she continued.

"I've got to reach Chambersburg this afternoon at the very latest. My daughter — Betsy — she's going to have her baby. When I bought my ticket they told me there might be delays, though. You know the raider — what's his name? Oh, yes! General Spurrier! Mad Jack Spurrier!" Again she shuddered. "Terrorizing folks up and down the valley the way he is! They say General Zwick has got ten thousand men chasing him!"

"Oh?" Charlie said, noncommittally. He was about to start on "Weeping Sad and Lonely," a favorite song among the troops, but she thumbed quickly through *Leslie's* to show him a woodcut of the redheaded Scourge of the Shenandoah. "There! Ain't he a cruel sight, with them narrow little cat's-eyes!"

Charlie had been too busy fleeing the capital to keep up with the news. "Well," he said, "I do hope they catch him, ma'am."

"Now what?" Adjusting her spectacles, she peered forward. The door banged open and the conductor was calling from the vestibule.

"Just sit tight, folks! The Army wants to make a little inspection!"

Fanning himself with his hat, a fat man near the door snarled, "What in Tophet *fur?* We're late already!"

The conductor shrugged. "Who knows why the dinged Army does *anything?*"

The old lady whispered to Charlie, "I vow they're looking for spies!"

He jumped, swallowed hard. "Yes, ma'am! Probably."

At the very least the Army would want to know why a well-set-up young man like Charlie Callaway wasn't in the war, serving his nation. Putting away the sweet potato, he muttered something about being thirsty and strolled to the water-butt at the opposite end of the car. As he was drinking from the dipper, a yellow-chevroned sergeant entered the far end, carrying a sheaf of papers. Charlie tried to appear casual, hooking one thumb in the pocket of his new flowered waistcoat; twelve dollars' worth of expensive tailoring from Dinwiddie's, on the Avenue. Damn! His valise was still in the overhead rack; he could not retrieve it without exciting suspicion. From the corner of his eye he observed the sergeant going through the wallet of the protesting fat man. Quietly he cracked the door of the rear vestibule, slipping his lean form through the opening. On the platform he scanned the file of cars ahead, outlines wavering in the August heat. When he stepped down, his boots crunched loudly in the cinders.

"Halt! You there!"

He froze. Leaning from an open window ahead, a hard-eyed soldier pointed a musket.

"Oh, Lord," Charlie muttered.

For a moment the soldier took his eyes off Charlie to yell at someone inside. "Sarge, there's this yahoo out here on the tracks and —"

Charlie dived into the greenery lining the rails. The musket boomed; clipped-off leaves sprayed his face. Rolling headlong, he sailed through a thicket of sumac and heard a dismal rip as the newly tailored pants lost a battle with a snag. Gathering speed, he caromed into space. Flapping his arms like a bird, he dropped into the river, swollen and muddy from summer rains. Bowled along by the current and sinking, ironically weighed down by expensive clothing, he thought of what Lorna said that day she broke off their engagement: "Charles Chaney Callaway, you'll come to a sad end, mark my words!" Right now he couldn't think of a more sad end than to drown in a Pennsylvania river with over a thousand dollars in greenbacks sewn into a flowered silk waistcoat.

No athlete, he fought to keep his head above water. The harder he paddled the deeper he sank. Less and less was he able to suck air into tortured lungs. After a while a mood of near-resignation came on him. He always figured the odds on every proposition; he was a born gambler. If the odds weren't good he never

4

bucked the house. Gurgling, he sank into the stream. The waters closed over his pomaded head, and a strange peacefulness enveloped him. So this is how it ends, he thought.

Faintly he detected strains of music. As from a great distance he saw himself toiling up a flight of stairs wrapped in drifts of diaphanous clouds. At the top of the stairs was a gate.

"Hello!" Charlie shouted.

There was no answer. He took out his sweet potato and blew a tender chord of supplication. An old man with a long beard looked over the gate.

"I'm Charlie Callaway."

Who?

"Callaway! Charles C."

The Old Gentleman leafed through a book. *Hmmmm — Caldwell, Callahan — here it is*. Taking off gold-rimmed spectacles, he rubbed the bridge of his nose. *What you want, Charlie?*

"I want in!"

Putting on the spectacles again, the Old Gentleman scanned the book, bony finger following the lines.

"This *is* Heaven, isn't it?" Charlie demanded.

Yep. The Old Gentleman continued to read. Finally he looked up. *Lorna left you, didn't she?*

Charlie blew spit from the sweet potato and put it in his pocket. "Well, Lorna was a very spiritual woman. She was big on good works. Volunteered to nurse in the hospitals and knitted socks for the soldiers — things like that. I guess I disappointed her. I meant well, though. I always meant well."

The Old Gentleman's face was stern. *Meant well? Hah! You're a gambling man, ain't you? Bet on anything! Full of tricks! Risk the happiness of your future bride! I don't blame Lorna for handing you your walking papers!*

Charlie was indignant. "Believe me, I tried! You see, her parents died, so she came out from her home in San Francisco to stay with a cousin in Baltimore. I met her when she got employment at the Patent Office. I'd just gone in to bring them a model of a — well, a mechanical device — when —"

A mechanical device! The Old Gentleman snickered. *A holdout, isn't that what it's called? A gadget to slip an ace out of your sleeve when you need one?*

"That isn't what I called it," Charlie said. "In the application I referred to it as a —"

I know the whole cheap story, the Old Gentleman interrupted, shaking his head. *I know all about you, you tinhorn! It's right here in this book. Shall I read on, Charlie Callaway?*

Charlie became angry. "Look here — you're not giving me any odds at all!" he complained.

Odds? We don't give odds up here, sinner! The Old Gentleman gestured, and lightning split the cerulean vault. Thunder rolled, deafening Charlie. Suddenly craven, he cowered. The Old Gentleman's words, amplified as if he were speaking through an enormous trumpet, shook him like an autumn leaf in a gale.

If it was time for your end, you miserable creature, I'd take pleasure in pulling this here lever and dropping you through the trapdoor to everlasting fires of sulphur and brimstone! But it ain't time — not quite! Now you just turn around, Callaway, and march down them golden stairs! Quick — make a flat shirt-tail out of here before you contaminate the premises! Reaching overhead, the Old Gentleman picked out a forked branch of lightning and hurled it at Charlie. *Scat!*

Panic-striken, Charlie turned. Losing his footing, he fell headlong down the golden stairs, arms and legs flung wide in an effort to stay himself.

"Oh, Lord!" he moaned. "I meant well! I always meant well! It was just that —"

As he fell another bolt grazed him and he bawled in terror. "Don't hit me with lightning! Please don't! I repent!"

Suddenly he seemed to come to rest, and he became aware of a gentle reciprocating motion; to and fro, to and fro. He surged back and forth, like the cars on the Northern Central that had lately borne him westward. It was not at all unpleasant, almost like being rocked in a cradle. A thought crossed his confused mind. Perhaps he was being reborn, given a new chance.

"No one ain't hitting you!" a harsh voice grumbled.

Opening his eyes, he looked up, trying to see his new papa or whoever it was. The vision was dim and bleary.

"What in hell you repenting *of?*" another voice demanded.

Charlie's stomach wrenched, and he gave up a great deal of river water.

A brawny hand took a grip of his coat and hoisted him like a side of beef on a meat hook. Squinting, he made out an evil bearded face. His good coat ripped; three packs of Steamboat playing cards fell out.

"Well," someone said. "We got us a gambling man, fellers!"

"Look, Slink!" another voice cried, astonished. "Money! Jesus Christ — look at the money sticking out of his vest!"

Swaying on his feet, ankle-deep in water riffling over the sandbar, Charlie peered at the blue-clad soldiers, hard-bitten regular cavalry. Laughing, they ripped his clothing further and helped themselves to his hard-earned funds.

"No!" he croaked, batting feebly at the clawing hands. "Stop it! Don't take my money!"

Someone gave him a shove and he fell backward over the barrel they had lately been rolling him over. The bearlike corporal, the one called Slink, face made more evil by a cast in one eye, leered. "Hell, if me and Pete and Homer hadn't saw you drifting down the river, you wouldn't have had no use for this money anyway — now would you, stranger?"

Charlie discovered he had lost a boot, too. He wiggled his toes in a wet sock and murmured, "Well —"

"What's going on here?" a nasal voice demanded.

Slink came to attention; the others followed suit.

"We kotched a spy, lieutenant! Me and Pete and Homer saw him swimming across the river, trying to escape to the Rebs!"

"A spy, eh, Slink?" The lieutenant was a cadaverous man with a black felt hat pinned rakishly up in the style of Louis Kossuth, the Hungarian patriot who had visited the United States and espoused the cause of the Union. "You, sir!" He addressed Charlie while retrieving bank notes from the disappointed soldiers. "What's your name?"

"Charles Callaway, sir."

"What in hell you doing with all this money?"

Lorna always said she could tell when Charlie was lying by the way he refused to look at her. Remembering, he stood straight, eyeing the lieutenant, and spoke in a loud although somewhat waterlogged voice.

"Well, sir — I had me a little house out near the Chain Bridge and I sold it to a widow woman. Her husband was a flour merchant and left her pretty well off, so she paid cash. I was just on my way to buy a dry-goods store in Springfield, Illinois, when —"

"You're lying," the lieutenant said in his flat ugly voice. Rolling the bills into a cylinder, he wrung water from them. "You're the one jumped the train up above when the patrol stopped it, isn't that right?" He didn't wait for an answer. "You men! Fix bayonets and form a guard detail! Keep an eye on the prisoner! He's one of Spurrier's agents!" He drew his saber and smacked Charlie across the rump. "Get going, reb! I'm taking you direct to Major Cairns. *Hup*, two, three, four!"

Limping, Charlie staggered up the hill surrounded by bayonets. Stones bruised his unbooted foot and his stomach gurgled and roiled. After a while they came to a tent where a square-cut blocky man was shaving at a tin mirror tied to a tree. Eyeing them, he asked, "Who in hell you got there, Hopkins?"

"A spy, sir. One of Spurrier's agents."

"I am not!" Charlie objected. "I'm a peaceful citizen, traveling to —"

"Look here!" Hopkins interrupted, holding out the bills. "See — a Confederate fiver, and there's more sprinkled throughout!"

Charlie swallowed hard. He should have examined the packets of bills more closely; he had been cheated.

"What are you doing with all this money?" the major demanded.

Charlie started again on the widow story. "You see, her husband was a lawyer — and left her quite a lot of money when he passed away —"

"You said he was a flour merchant!" the lieutenant snarled.

"Well," Charlie amended, "that was her *first* husband!"

"A pack of lies," Major Cairns sighed, wiping soap from his face. "Search him, Hopkins."

While the major trimmed his burnsides the cavalrymen seized Charlie roughly, as if it were his fault the lieutenant had taken away their money. They stripped him until he stood almost naked, shivering not with cold but fear, the abject remnant of a once handsome and well-dressed human being. Cowering, his six feet two inches was reduced to considerably less. He had never been a brave man, eschewing violence in all forms, especially that directed at him. Shaking, teeth chattering, he decided to tell the truth.

"Uh — that m-m-money — it's from an enlistment bounty. I — well, *three* enlistment bounties."

That was the truth. After Lorna had spurned him, his luck had gone incredibly bad. Pockets empty and holes in his shoes, he had collected three enlistment bounties under three different names, none of them his own. It had been easy; the newspapers were full of advertisements:

Wanted: a substitute to go in a first-rate Pennsylvania company of infantry. A gentleman whose health is impaired will give a fair price for a substitute. Apply immediately at Willard's Hotel, Room No. 17, between the hours of ten and three o'clock."

Well, his health had been impaired, too, hadn't it — his financial health? If the fools were that free with their money, why not take it? It would teach them a beneficial lesson, bribing other citizens to shoulder *their* burdens! He felt almost virtuous.

"That was dishonest," he admitted, "and I'm ready to take my medicine. Only I'm not a spy, you understand. I —"

No one was paying any attention to him.

"What's this?" The lieutenant held up a piece of spring steel shaped like a clothespin. Actually, it was a device Charlie had made to better the odds in a stud game; he called it his "bug," and it had stung many players. A metal clip, points sharpened, held a critical ace when the bug was pushed into the underside of a wooden table in proximity to his vest. Someday, when he perfected his dream holdout, such a crude and dangerous device would be only a historical curiosity. "It's a kind of toothpick I invented," he lied. "Two points, see? Gets both sides of a tooth at once."

"What's this?" The lieutenant held up Charlie's ocarina, warily, as if it were an explosive device.

11

"Sweet potato! I — I play it! For amusement, you know!"

The lieutenant placed the ocarina on the ground, stamped on it with a booted foot. Charlie quailed as it smashed into splinters. Hopkins, examining the wreckage, said, "Don't appear there's no secret messages in here, major."

"He's a smart one, though," the major observed, sitting on a stump. He crossed his legs and lighted a cigar. "What's that?"

The lieutenant handed him a folded piece of paper he had extracted from Charlie's trousers. Major Cairns spread it out, hooked spectacles over his ears, and stared at the damp paper. "All kinds of little squiggles. Probably a map of our brigade dispositions."

"That's just a bill!" Charlie protested. "The ink's run on it and made those little squiggles! That's a statement from Dinwiddie's, on the Avenue, for some clothes they made for me!" He had not paid Dinwiddie, and did not care to go into detail. "Please — I'm a sporting gentleman down on his luck, that's all! I was just going to — this is the Lord's truth — to join up with Nathan Goodbody in St. Louis! He taught me the trade, see? He and I used to work the riverboats and he wrote me St. Louis was full of easy marks, so that's where I was headed for. Don't you understand?"

Flipping his coattails to clear his saber, the major rose. "You've got more stories than a hound dog's got fleas! What you are is one of that devil Spurrier's agents, it's plain to see. You're a smooth article, and have probably got secret information on you somewhere

12

right now even if we can't locate it!" Chewing the cigar, he growled an order to Lieutenant Hopkins. "Take him out and shoot him!"

"Shoot me?" Charlie's voice broke into falsetto. "But I told you the truth! I mean — well, there may be a few details that are inaccurate, but —"

Gleefully Slink and Pete and Homer seized him, dragged him away. "My congressman is going to hear about this!" he protested, forgetting that as a resident of the District he had no congressman.

"Take him a good piece downriver!" the major called. "I don't like to hear these things!"

With Charlie struggling and arguing, Corporal Slink and Pete and Homer bore him back to the river and forced him at bayonet point to stand still. They propped him before a sycamore tree and lined up expectantly.

This can't be happening to me, Charlie thought in panic, brushing away a bluebottle fly. It just can't! I'm too young to die!

"Load!" the lieutenant commanded.

The soldiers fumbled for cartridges, tore them open with their teeth, poured powder into the barrels of the muskets. They unwrapped lead balls, dropped them into the bores and rammed them home, replacing the rammers in the clips under the barrels. The odds were rapidly dropping.

"Listen," Charlie pleaded, "this is a mistake! Can't we talk this over?"

There was a chorus of clicks, hard and deadly against the rushing of the river, as the soldiers pulled the hammers back to half cock and pressed percussion cartridges onto the nipples.

"Ready?" the lieutenant inquired, raising his saber.

"Good Lord!" Charlie babbled, sinking to his knees. "Just a dentist, that's all! Honor graduate of Dr. Motherwell's College of Dentistry and Animal Husbandry! For a while I had an office on Connecticut Avenue, in Washington. 'Painless extractions, fillings of precious metals —'"

Hopkins stared at him. "You telling the truth, or is this just another story?"

Charlie raised his hand. "As God is my witness, sir! It's the truth! You see, Lorna wouldn't marry me until I made something out of myself! So I went to Dr. Motherwell's College, took the whole six months' course and did well, if I do say so myself. But I wouldn't give up gambling, and my practice kind of dwindled, and finally she said to me, 'Charlie, you'll never change! I'm going home to San Francisco.' So I —"

"Why didn't you say so before?"

"Say what?"

"That you were a dentist!"

"No one asked me!"

Corporal Slink protested. "Ain't we going to shoot him, lieutenant?"

"No. Not yet, anyway." Hopkins prodded Charlie with the saber. "Up the hill again!" The lieutenant hummed a little tune as they clambered up, even helping Charlie when he stumbled his stockinged toe

14

on a root and sprawled flat. Charlie was puzzled. Still, he had not been shot — so far.

Major Cairns was excited when he heard the news, chewing his cigar into tatters.

"I thought you'd like to know, sir," Lieutenant Hopkins said, modestly adding, "I drug it out of him, sir."

"Yes," the major said. "By Jesus Christ, yes! This *is* an interesting development!"

"With the major's permission, sir, I'll just take the prisoner along to the general's headquarters and —"

"Like hell you will! That is — I mean to say — well done and all that, Hopkins, but you're in charge of the river patrol. I'll just take our dentist along myself."

"But, sir —"

"Don't worry! I'll see you get proper recognition."

Hopkin's face was as black as his hat. Sulkily, he turned away.

"You three men," the major ordered, "surround the prisoner and follow me!"

Briskly he clambered through the underbrush, cutting weeds with his saber. Charlie followed meekly. The guards ambled behind, talking in low tones.

"So that's the ticket!"

"Ole major ain't no fool, is he?"

"General Zwick going to make him a colonel for this!" Slink snorted with laughter, then broke off as Major Cairns looked back.

"What you figure Lieutenant Hopkins to get out of this?" Pete asked in a low voice.

"A big naught with a hole in it!" Homer giggled, and in a fit of humor prodded Charlie on the backside with his bayonet. "Git goin', dentist! Ole general cain't hardly wait!"

Brigade headquarters was a long way back. Generals, Charlie surmised, did not care to get close to the fighting. They must have marched two miles or more before they came to a cluster of Sibley tents in a field of poppies, high on a tree-studded bluff. Horses tied to trees whinnied and bit at flies. Gold-braided staff colonels pored over maps spread on wooden tables and drank coffee. A flag with a shiny star fluttered on a staff over a larger tent, and a sentry barred their way.

"Who goes there?" The sentry was a fresh-faced boy, typical, Charlie thought, of the children now being drafted for the damned war.

"Put down that gun! Major Henry Cairns, Tenth Illinois, with important information for General Zwick!"

Jealous of delegated authority, the boy demanded, "Who's the prisoner, then?"

"Oh, Jesus!" Cairns thrust him aside and halted at attention before the general's tent, saluting. "General, sir?" he called.

An aide poked his head out. "The general's having his breakfast."

"This is important!"

The aide withdrew, and after a moment opened the tent flap again. "Come in."

While the major conferred with the general Charlie took off his sock and examined his sore foot. Hastily he drew on the sock when Cairns emerged.

16

"All right, you! Inside!"

The brigade commander's tent was hot and musty, feebly lighted by sun filtering through the patched canvas. On a keg sat General Zwick, moodily dipping hardtack into a cup of coffee. The only other furniture was a wooden table littered with maps and a field cot.

"This is the prisoner, sir," Major Cairns explained.

"Spy, eh?" The general was a pudgy man with a plump pink face and a pate over which had been arranged a few strands of white hair. "Dentist, too, *hein?*" The voice was heavily Teutonic.

"Dentist — yes, sir," Charlie admitted. "No spy, though! You see, I had a practice in Washington. 'Prices for any pocketbook,' and then when Lorna —"

"*Ja, ja!*" General Zwick groaned. Reaching into his mouth, he drew out a chunk of bone-hard issue bread which had not softened in the coffee and flung it away with an oath. "*Mein Gott* — I have bad teeth, you know! All the Zwicks have bad teeth; *grossvater, grossmutter,* papa, mama, cousins, uncles — all!"

"I'm sorry," Charlie apologized.

"You fix my teeth, *hein?*"

So this was what it was all about! "Well," Charlie said, "I'm a dentist — a good dentist."

Groaning, the general struggled up from the keg to approach Charlie, mouth tugged wide by two plump fingers. "How I suffer! When my teeth ache that devil Spurrier could have me without a fight! Look in there, dentist! What you see?"

Major Cairns was shocked when Charlie took hold of the general's high-ranking arm in a familiar way and moved him about so a shaft of sunlight through a pinhole in the tent illumined the mouth. Charlie, although used to such phenomena, recoiled.

"What means this, hmmm?" General Zwick asked, collapsing on the keg.

"Well, sir, you've got a very bad mouth, as we dentists say," Charlie explained, feeling a smallish surge of hope. Then the small hope flattened out and disappeared. His dentist's kit — instruments, ether, all — had been in the valise abandoned on the railway train. "However," he added, "I — well, you see, I came away in such a hurry I left all my instruments behind."

The general let out an animal snarl of pain. "Cairns, take him out and shoot him!"

"Wait a minute!" Charlie protested. "Let's talk this over, can't we?"

The general, holding his aching jaw, scowled. "You fix my teeth?"

"I fix your teeth — sir," Charlie promised, desperate to improve the odds, his own teeth tending to chatter, and a cold leaden sensation developing in the pit of his stomach. He didn't know how he was going to do it, but he had no choice. Still, he had always been handy with his hands, making many of his own picks and probes and forceps. The skill had been burnished by his long search for the ultimate holdout, the ideal contrivance of cords, pulleys, and oiled joints to be worn under the vest and down one arm, under the sleeve, terminating in a delicate claw to push a valuable card into a palm. In spite of all his skill and ingenuity, however, his efforts had not yet worked very well.

18

"Yes," he repeated, trying to sound confident. "I fix your teeth, all right, general! But you'll have to give me a little time!"

"How long, dentist?" The general's eye was stony.

Charlie took a guess. "If I can have the services of some of the facilities of your command — say two hours."

The general waved a free hand. "You and your detail take him away, Cairns! Giff him whateffer he wants!"

"A farrier, say, with a forge —"

"All right, dentist! Go! *Schnell!* I am suffering terrible!"

Major Cairns cleared his throat. "Sir, do you think a corporal and two privates is an appropriate command for a regular army major? I mean —"

"Are you being insubordinate?"

"No, sir!" the major said hastily.

As Cairns motioned Charlie to the doorflap the general called a warning. "Whateffer you do, don't shoot him till he fix my teeth! If he is harmed, I swear — me, Brigadier General Peter Zwick — to personal rip those oak leaves off your shoulders! *Verstehen Sie?*"

Major Cairns blanched. "Yes, *sir!*"

Outside, Slink and Pete and Homer put away their cards — Charlie's cards — and scrambled up. "We going to shoot him now, sir?" Slink demanded.

What was it Hamlet said? "There is nothing either good or bad but thinking makes it so." Charlie refused to think anymore on the bad. After all, he was — at least for the present — General Peter Zwick's protégé, and not to be summarily shot. The odds against him were awful, he had to admit, but he meant to act as if they were a lead-pipe cinch.

"Find me a farrier, major," he said, a brisk note of command in his voice.

"What?"

"General's orders," Charlie said firmly. "Let's go. *Hup*, two, three, four!"

CHAPTER
TWO

Though orphaned almost at birth in San Francisco, Lorna Bascomb had never seen the city's sprawling Chinatown. Now that she had returned from her unhappy experience in the nation's capital to live with Uncle Matthew and Aunt Carrie, her uncle was anxious to show her his Christian Mission to the Chinese in Brooklyn Alley. For years he had been a Methodist minister. Now retired, Reverend Hewitt still devoted himself unstintingly to good works; he was over seventy years of age but still alert and active. He described Chinatown to Lorna as they walked.

"A city in itself, Niece, filled with ugliness and disease and vice. Yet the Chinese are basically good people — thrifty and industrious. I hope my small efforts will someday give them the dignity and respect that they have been denied."

In San Francisco the general area of Sacramento Street and Dupont Street was known as Little China, a place of gambling, prostitution, and opium dreams. Slave girls imported from Shanghai and Canton were used, reused, and finally, beauty fled, abandoned to beg. Opium was the only relase from drudgery, misery, and poverty for the laundryman or eating-house cook.

Exploited by their own people, the Chinese were also looked down on by white citizens.

At Waverly Place and Washington Street was Little Pete's gambling house and headquarters from which he ran his Oriental satrapy with all the power and majesty of a Manchurian emperor. Each evening expensive carriages rolled down the crowded avenues full of white men eager to visit the high-class gambling establishments and parlor-houses controlled by Little Pete, the King of the Tongs. Ah Toy and Suey Sin were Little Pete's chief madames. The parlors of their Palaces of Delight were richly furnished with teak and bamboo furniture, embroidered wall-hangings, soft couches, and cushions of finest silk.

On the upper floors of the garish red and yellow building, eaves slanting upward to keep evil spirits from sliding down, to Little Pete's palatial headquarters came the leaders of San Francisco society — prominent civic officials, senior officers from the Presidio — to play poker, baccarat, roulette, or whatever pleased their fancy. Pausing before the building, Lorna's Uncle Matthew pointed.

"There is the headquarters of Fung Jin Toy, better known as Little Pete. He is an evil man who does nothing to help his miserable countrymen! Most of the poverty, the vice, the suffering you see here can be laid at the door of Little Pete. I have often remonstrated with him, but to no avail."

The King of the Tongs so far did not see a threat in Matthew Hewitt's efforts to better the situation of the Chinese, especially the situation of the imported slave girls; the minister's efforts were obviously unsuccessful anyway. "White folks like China girls!" He had leered at Reverend Hewitt in his palatial suite. "You no do good, revvum, but go ahead — fine!" He had grinned, sucked again at the gurgling opium pipe. "Little Pete fair — no?"

As her uncle related the tale, Lorna was puzzled. Shrinking as they passed an ominous-looking column of burly Chinese in black clothing almost like uniforms — *boo how doy*, her uncle explained, hatchet men for the tongs — she clutched Reverend Hewitt's arm more tightly. "How does he manage to do this — to be so dishonest and cruel, and yet prosper?"

"Little Pete is hand in glove with the politicians in city hall! He is an inveterate gambler and plays high-stakes poker with the aldermen and chief of police every Thursday."

"But is there no champion for these people?"

"None — except perhaps for my poor efforts."

On their way to the mission they paused for a moment at the corner of Washington Street just north of Kearney. Below them was a kind of huge cellar, opening on an underground court into which denizens of the place descended by means of rickety ladders. It was an enormous anthill swarming with black-clad Orientals shuffling about in tattered slippers. Some carried laundry in baskets suspended from both ends of a kind of yoke that fitted across the shoulders. Others hurried containers of food and pots of tea to workingmen's restaurants. Beggars crouched along the walls, wailing entreaties and holding out tin cups.

Huddled bodies lay about in the scanty autumn sunshine, senseless from opium. Naked children, bony and undernourished, cried with thin desperate sounds while ragged mothers tried to comfort them. From the depths rose a stench of excrement, rotting food, sweat, laundry steam, the odor of what Uncle Matthew said was opium; it laced the air with a nauseating thread of sweetness.

"Though some of our more facetious journalists refer to this as the Palace Hotel," Uncle Matthew explained, "its proper name is the Devil's Kitchen. That is what it is — a hell on earth where the Devil cooks his evil stews! This is where poor slave girls go when they are no longer young, no longer beautiful, no longer desired, when they're worn out, broken, diseased — they come here to die in a squalid room in a squalid bed." Suddenly wrathful, he raised fists above his head. "My Lord, my dear Lord — how can you allow this?"

Lorna pressed her cheek against the lapel of his shabby coat. Uncle Matthew used most of the funds he collected for the mission and spent little on himself.

"You will prevail, I know, Uncle," she comforted him. "Good always triumphs in the end!"

He patted her hand. "I hope the Lord will forgive my outbreak! He sees the sparrow's fall, we all know that! Still, while it is a most un-Christian thought, from time to time I imagine a bolt of heavenly lightning striking down Little Pete and Suey Sin and Ah Toy and all the procurers and pimps — a bolt of such power that it would burn out vice and corruption and give us a cleansed and refreshed city!"

24

Lorna and her uncle stood before the shabby whitewashed wooden structure in Brooklyn Alley that was the Christian Mission to the Chinese. Little more than a shed — it was originally a livery stable — it was rented by Reverend Hewitt for five dollars a month from Little Pete. Here he and a few Chinese helpers daily cooked food for beggars; sewed up cuts; administered ipecac, blue mass, and stomach bitters to the ill and injured; and labored to convert the Orientals to Christianity.

"But they are remarkably stubborn," he sighed. "They take it as their lot to be unhappy, and believe that in another life they will be rich and happy."

Despite her Aunt Carrie's objections, Reverend Hewitt had this morning allowed Lorna to accompany him. Aunt Carrie had been aghast.

"Surely, Matthew, you're not going to allow an innocent orphan girl to go into that horrible neighborhood!"

Lorna was insistent. "Auntie, I *must* go! I have been a burden to you and Uncle for several weeks now, without turning my hand, and it is time I did useful work! Besides, I am not so innocent!"

Both looked at her askance. "Innocent?" Aunt Carrie asked in a shocked voice. "My dear child, you are not — innocent?"

Blushing, Lorna explained, "I do not mean it in the way it perhaps sounded! All I mean is that I have traveled East, 'seen the elephant' as they say there, been engaged to a young man, and am not a child any longer, dear Auntie!"

The three ramshackle rooms of the mission were already crowded with supplicants. A wizened old woman named Dah Pah Tsin was Matthew Hewitt's assistant, keeping order among the thronging Chinese with a tattered umbrella and a torrent of Chinese invective.

"There, there!" Uncle Matthew said. "That will do, Dah Pah Tsin! I am here, and will take over." In the midst of the throng who were pulling at his coat, clutching his hands, and pouring entreaties into his ear, he gestured to Lorna. "Go with Dah Pah Tsin. She will need help with the noon meal. God be thanked, child, for your offer of help, which is sorely needed!"

Under the old lady's direction Lorna tied her hair with a ribbon, rolled up her sleeves, and dumped ingredients into an iron pot simmering over a wood fire in the yard behind the mission. For the most part the vegetables were scavenged cabbages and carrots and tomatoes thrown away at the produce market. This day one of the Chinese helpers had found several overripe chickens thrown out in an alley. Holding her nose, Lorna cut them up and dropped them into the stew.

"Cook long time, no smell bad!" Dah Pah Tsin laughed, seeing Lorna wrinkle her nose at the odor.

At noon they served over a hundred poor at the mission. When there was only a little broth and a few shreds of chicken skin at the bottom of the iron pot, Dah Pah Tsin brought a bowl to Reverend Hewitt, along with a ball of rice. Aunt Carrie had prepared a packet of lunch; when Lorna offered a sandwich, Reverend Hewitt shook his head. "That is for you, child!"

"But, Uncle —"

"I must eat what the Lord has allowed for these poor heathen."

After that she found the chicken sandwiches, celery, and chocolate cake to be sawdust in her mouth. Later she gave most of the lunch away, piece by piece, to the swarm of slant-eyed urchins who followed her about as she swept the bare dirt-floored room where services were to be held later.

"I know," her uncle admitted, "that few hold with my idea of feeding them first, thinking instead the food ought to be a bribe to entice them to the Lord. But I don't see it that way. If they come to the arms of our Redeemer, I want them to come because of his boundless love, and not because their stomachs are empty."

The services were scantily attended with no more than fifteen or twenty Chinese, mostly old men and women, inscrutable on the rickety chairs, nail kegs, and wooden benches. Uncle Matthew started strong, voice filled with conviction and hope. As black-clad figures rose and slipped out into the autumn sun, one at a time, he sighed, sang a final hymn accompanied only by Lorna's hesitant soprano, and gave up.

"I am not reaching them!" he complained. "I am failing in the Lord's work!"

It was nearing sunset when Lorna blew out the lamp on Reverend Hewitt's desk in the tiny cubbyhole off the "chapel" and rolled down her sleeves. She was exhausted but content in a way she had not been since the debacle of her engagement to Charlie Callaway.

"Uncle," she said, coming behind him where he sat, dejected, at the old desk, and kissing his bald spot, "I have made a decision. I hope you — and Auntie too — will approve it. I want to —"

He sat up. "Eh? What was that?"

"I was only saying —"

"No, no! That — sound!"

She listened, hearing a faint scraping at the door. "I — I don't know. I will go and see."

"No, child. Stay here." Warily he went to the barred door, listened. "Who is there?"

The sound was no human voice; it mewled. Reverend Hewitt spoke in singsong Cantonese. Finally he unbarred the door.

On the sill knelt a small and fragile figure, wrapped in the remnants of what had once been an expensive brocaded gown. The upturned grimy face was beseeching.

"Come up," Uncle Matthew urged, and helped the crouching figure to stand. He shook his head in compassion. "Who are you?"

The ragged figure sagged in his arms, head wagging helplessly.

Between them they carried the slight figure to one of the chairs. Lorna brought lukewarm leftover tea, and the girl sipped it while Uncle Matthew interrogated her in Cantonese.

"She has been beaten!" Lorna pointed out indignantly, dabbing a cut under the girl's eye with her handkerchief. "And she is thin as a rail!"

"A prostitute. An old story!"

"A — a prostitute?" Lorna was horrified.

28

"Loi San says she is fourteen. Little Pete lost her in a game of fan tan."

Lorna swallowed hard, and put a trembling hand to her lips. "Dear Jesus! The evils of gambling!"

"She — she is diseased, too, I am afraid. Do you see the sores on her cheeks, her forehead?"

Lorna was almost too sickened to speak. "Fourteen." she murmured. "I cannot believe it! She looks like an old woman!"

Her uncle went to the kitchen, came back with some chicken scraps and a crust which he wrapped in an old copy of the *Chronicle*. Fumbling in a pocket, he took out a few coins and handed them, along with the package, to the girl. Lorna had the feeling it was all the money her uncle had.

"This is the most I can do for now," Reverend Hewitt said gently. "Come back tomorrow, at noon, for food. Maybe the Lord will send us manna again — who knows?"

"But, Uncle —"

He spread his arms wide. "It is hard, but what else can I do, Lorna? She is only one of many!"

Bowing painfully, the girl backed away from them, clutching the package. A moment later she disappeared into the growing dusk.

"Someday," Reverend Hewitt muttered, "the Lord will bless me with some money! When that time comes I swear to make a hospital here — a refuge and home for these poor girls! In the meantime —" He sighed, motioned to Lorna. "We must be getting home. Your aunt will be worried about us."

That night, in the glow of the Argand lamp, Lorna talked with Aunt Carrie. Her uncle, weary and discouraged, had gone to bed.

"Auntie, I have found my niche!" She was excited. "While I am grateful to you and Uncle for taking me in, I feel also I must do something to repay you. I want to work for Uncle Matthew at the mission!"

Her aunt was shocked, peering over iron-rimmed spectacles.

"My dear child —"

"Please, Auntie! I am not a child!"

"But — that awful area! Beggars, assassins, thieves, prostitutes —"

"I know all that. Still, I am determined!"

Aunt Carrie laid down her knitting. "Are you sure this is a reasoned reaction? I mean, after your unhappy experience back East?"

Though her aunt was dear to her a note of exasperation came into Lorna's voice. "That has nothing to do with it!"

Her aunt's voice was concerned but kindly. "You still love him, I think. What's his name? Charlie?"

"Charlie Callaway, Auntie." Lorna bit her lip. Charlie, oh, Charlie! She remembered the night in Washington, she and Charlie swinging on the porch of her boarding-house on F Street, right around the corner from the War Department building where Mr. Lincoln came in the evening to read dispatches from the field. Charlie had played his sweet potato; even now the softly silken notes lingered in her ear. Charlie sang, too, and quoted Shakespeare so beautifully! Oh, Charlie, what bliss we could have shared if you had only given up your evil gambling!

"Are you sure you're not just — well, plunging into something to forget?"

"Of course I'm sure! I mean — well, a young woman needs a rewarding activity! What better thing than to do the Lord's work helping Uncle Matthew? I am penniless, you know, but strong and healthy!"

Aunt Carrie resumed her knitting. "Well, we will see! In the morning, before Matthew goes to the mission, we will discuss it."

Taking her aunt's hand and pressing it to her cheek, Lorna rose. "Thank you! You will not be sorry, nor will Uncle Matthew!"

In her bedroom at the modest home in the Western Addition she put on a nightgown and sat at the open window, feeling the night envelop her in a velvet cloak. To the east the city lights burned, but here it was quiet, peaceful. Crickets chirped; delicate and spicy, a scent of jasmine came to her from the trellis under the window. In the west a cheese-yellow rind of moon hovered over the fog bank that would soon envelop the city.

Charlie! Oh, Charlie! As she thought of him, her body trembled and she felt an unmaidenly stimulation. Charlie Callaway, so gentle and handsome with his curly black hair, blue eyes — the long sensitive delicate fingers, like those of an artist. She loved Charlie, but she did not think she ever really knew him. Somehow he seemed always to be playing a role, holding himself out, holding back the real and true Charlie Callaway whom she knew to be good and kind and honorable. It was almost as if he dared not trust himself, the *real* Charlie, but had to depend on subterfuge. His gambling had been like that; a desperate hope that a big strike, a run of luck, would bring him what hard work brought other people. She stared at the moon, but the scalloped vision dimmed through the tears in her eyes. Charlie, didn't you love me enough? Almost she could feel his hand holding hers as they sat in Rock Creek Park of a Sunday while he read sonnets to her. Then, suddenly annoyed at such romantic thoughts, she went to her bed, turned back the coverlet. On her knees she prayed for the poor little prostitute Loi San, and felt better.

The farrier sergeant, paring a hoof preparatory to nailing a shoe on a bay mare, was angry when Charlie Callaway started searching through the tools laid out on his bench in an abandoned shack.

"Hey, you! What the hell you think you're doin'?"

"I need a good stout pair of pliers!"

"Well, go someplace else and look! Them is my personal tools!"

Undaunted, Charlie continued to rummage, finding a small pair used to pull horseshoe nails. "I'd like to borrow your grindstone, sergeant," he said. He bent over the wheel, one foot on the pedal that served to spin the grindstone.

With an oath the sergeant tossed a red-hot shoe back into the forge. "Get away from there or I'll bust you to flinderjigs!"

Charlie gestured to Major Cairns, standing sullenly nearby.

"Tell him, major."

"General's orders," Cairns grumbled. "He's to get anything he wants."

Carefully Charlie ground the jaws of the pliers down into a fair simulation of dental forceps. "Thanks," he said to the sergeant.

Hobbling on one boot, Charlie wandered through the camp. No ether, no chloroform; worrying out that stub of a tooth would be painful! His concern was increased when Major Cairns said, with some malice, "You hurt that old man with those horseshoe tongs and he's going to be mighty mad! He'll gallop down your throat and stomp your insides out!"

The popping of gunfire along the river increased. Slink and Pete and Homer peered through the trees in an effort to see what was going on. Major Cairns watched Charlie pulling up poppies already going to seed in the hot sun.

"God damn it, this is no time to pick daisies! Something's going on down there! What in hell —"

"These are poppies," Charlie explained. He remembered the time his Aunt Flora Bickford brewed tea from dried poppies and Uncle Willie slept for three days before Aunt Flora could wake him. "The Chinese make opium from them. Maybe Pennsylvania poppies will work the same way. Here are some funny-looking mushrooms, too. I'll put a few of them in."

"But what —"

"You'll see." Observing a sutler's wagon in a grove of sycamores, he wandered in that direction. Pausing before the wagon with its load of biscuits, candies, Lone Jack pipe tobacco, and items of clothing, he asked, "You got any bourbon whiskey?"

Seeing Major Cairns, the sutler shook his head vigorously. "General don't allow no licker in camp!"

"I'll wager," Charlie remarked, "that this man has under his counter a wide assortment of booze; rum, gin, whiskey, whatever. I need a bottle."

"What in hell do you need bourbon for?" the major demanded.

"I will also wager," Charlie said, "that if he doesn't bring out a bottle of at least corn whiskey, both he and you, major, are going to suffer when I report same to General Zwick. I need some alcohol to prepare the general properly."

Major Cairns ground his teeth. "All right!" Turning to the sutler, he said, "Give me a bottle of whiskey!"

Charlie twisted off the wire and pulled the cork, sampling the contents of the stone bottle. "Hmmm," he said professionally. "Good stuff! Prime medical grade!"

"That's a dollar!" the sutler said nervously.

"Pay him," Charlie instructed.

The major glowered. "I'll be damned if I —"

"You took all my money!"

Grumbling, the major dug in his pocket and tossed a rumpled greenback on the counter.

"You can always file a claim with the government after the war," Charlie pointed out.

In a cook tent he mashed the bulbous poppy pods and the mushrooms in a stoneware dish while the sweaty cooks watched. "A medical experiment," Charlie explained. Judiciously adding bourbon, he made a muddy paste.

"Hurry, damn it!" Major Cairns urged. "I've got to be getting back to the river before someone court-martials me!"

Charlie poured in more bourbon until the brew was the consistency of a thin soup. Borrowing a canteen, he filled it and rose.

"I am ready," he announced with dignity.

At the general's tent a crowd of staff officers milled about, worried. Charlie heard a colonel say, "Spurrier's broke through downriver!" Another officer contradicted him. "I heard he swam his horses across at Sawyer's Crossing!" A third, a burly captain chewing a stogie, said, "What in hell's wrong with the old man? Why don't he come out here and tell us what to do?"

The general was pacing the earthen floor of the tent in carpet slippers, moaning, head wrapped in a cloth. "*Lieber Gott*, I am in agony! It rumors that Spurrier is here, there, everywhere — and I am in such pain I cannot even think!" He grabbed Charlie by the shoulders and shook him. "*Ach*, help me, dentist!

With the major's help, Charlie stretched Zwick out on the wooden table, first brushing away the blizzard of maps. In his best professional manner he said, "Now you just rest easy, sir, and I'll bring an end to your suffering, which I must say you bear well!"

"You hurt me, dentist? Py jiminy — I can stand no more pain or I go crazy!"

Charlie shook up the contents of the canteen. "Just drink this, general."

"What is it?"

"A soothing compound I invented to ease suffering. A harmless anodyne, sir."

Muttering, the general took a mouthful, wincing as the liquid encountered his bad tooth.

"Try a little more, please."

General Zwick smacked his lips. "Not so bad. Tastes like *schnapps!*" He tipped up the canteen.

"Listen." Major Cairns muttered. "I've got to leave, Callison, or whatever your name is. Spurrier and his raiders will be in the Capitol unless someone does something. You're in charge here, see? Whatever happens is on your head! I'm leaving."

From the river Charlie could hear an almost continuous crackle of musketry. By this time he had hoped to be well on his way to Kansas City, yet here he was marooned in a tent with a suppurating molar. The Callaway luck was running out.

"Nice," the general murmured.

"Eh?"

"Dreams." General Zwick smiled beatifically. "I have nice dream now. Give me another swallow of that stuff, dentist!"

Charlie handed him the canteen, snatching it away as the general gargled down almost half. "That's enough!" he cried. "Good Lord! Now you just lay there, sir, and let it work. I'll have that bad tooth out quicker 'n an alligator can chew a puppy!"

The general lay flat; Charlie folded the dangling arms over his chest. Seeing the fixed grin and the glassy eyes, he felt panic. Had he given the old man too much? Quickly he bent over and listened to the chest; there was a reassuring thump.

"General!"

No answer; the patient was ready, if not over-ready.

With his fingers Charlie pried open the jaws and peered within the odorous cavern. It was still there, that blackened stub of a tooth. Carefully probing with the makeshift forceps, he tried to get a good grip. "Damn," he muttered; the general's slack jaws kept closing about the tool. Finally he took off one of the patient's carpet slippers and rolled it up, jamming it in the general's mouth to wedge open the jaws. In the dim heat of the tent he was sweating. Sweat ran down his cheeks and dripped on the general's brass-buttoned tunic. Outside, there were shouts and cries. He heard a pounding of hoofs, and a gun went off entirely too near the tent. He flinched, but continued to search for a purchase.

"Oh, *shit!*"

By now the jaws of the forceps must have mangled the general's gums, but there was no way out; he had to pull the damned tooth. Clenching his fist around the handles of the forceps, he clamped hard, hearing an unnerving crunch. Still, he had hold of the root! Cautiously he pulled, then harder. Something was coming! Panting, he pulled harder. Suddenly the rotting thing popped out. Charlie fell over backward,

37

triumphantly holding up the blackened stub with its wormlike roots.

"I've got it!" He scrambled up, shook the sleeping general. "Wake up! Look here, damn it all! I've got it!"

Peter Zwick continued recumbent. His face was pale, the smile fixed in a way that reminded Charlie uncomfortably of the way the undertakers had fixed up Aunt Zoë when she passed away from liver blight.

"General? Sir?" He shook the limp body. "For God's sake! Wake up!"

In panic he tore open the tunic, pressed his ear against the flannel shirt. Strain as he would, concentrating against the rattle of gunfire that seemed to surround the tent, he could hear no heartbeat. He staggered back, still holding the extracted molar aloft in this forceps. The poppy and bourbon mixture must have been too strong for the old man's heart!

"I've killed him!" he blurted. Fearful, guilty, he stared about. He was alone in the tent, alone with a corpse! First an embezzler of enlistment bounties, then a spy, now a murderer! Lorna had been right; oh, so right. This time he would probably be hanged instead of shot. His hand went to his neck and he felt it tenderly. The end, the end of a misspent life! Why hadn't he gone to Sunday school when his ma wanted him to?

"I'm lost," he muttered. "Lost in a sea of sin, and the boat's sinking!" Only dimly did he apprehend the pounding of hoofs outside. Not knowing what else to do, he pulled a rumpled sheet off the general's cot and spread it over the still form. Wasn't there some kind of prayer he could say? The body was cooling, the vital fire gone. Somewhere a soul was winging its way heavenward, unshriven.

He was trying to think of a psalm when the doorflap opened. A shaft of sunlight bored in, illuminating him in pitiless glare.

"I did it," he confessed. "Take me away! The wages of sin is death! That's in the Bible. Romans somewhere, I think."

At first the form in the doorway was only a dusty shadow, backlit by the sun. Then, squinting, Charlie made out details. The man was tall and lanky, clad in a dirty gray uniform with yellow piping; ropy red mustaches hung over his jowls. He held revolvers in each hand, and his eyes glittered with a hot yellow light, like those of a cat contemplating a platter of mice.

"Where is Peter Zwick?"

There was no doubt in Charlie's mind as to the action demanded of him. The intruder must be — was — the Confederate raider; Mad Jack Spurrier himself, the Scourge of the Shenandoah! In abject terror, Charlie turned to run.

CHAPTER
THREE

In his flight Charlie crashed headlong into the central pole of the Sibley tent. It skidded sideways; a cloud of moldy-smelling canvas descended. Trying to claw his way out, Charlie became more tightly swathed in the fallen tent. Thrashing about, he was aware of wild cries from outside, a rattle of gunfire, the neighing of a frightened horse.

"Help!" he shouted. "Help!"

Trying to free himself he fell to hands and knees. Something ripped the canvas near his cheek. He stared wild-eyed at a dot of daylight. A bullet had lately passed; the edges of the hole were singed by its heat. Frantically he redoubled his efforts to escape the clinging mantle. The doorflap! There was a doorflap. Where in hell was it? His groping hand found something. Desperately he snatched at it. A boot struck out and hit him in the head. Dazed, he heard an angry voice yell, "God damn it, let go!"

In the gloom Charlie stared into the cat-green eyes of Mad Jack Spurrier; together they were trapped under the fallen tent. With no thought other than to save himself, Charlie wrapped his arms about the lank form

40

of the raider. Rolling about in the folds of canvas, Spurrier howled, "Let me go, I said! God damn it —"

Charlie screamed for help. "Jesus, won't somebody come?" Like a leech he clung to Spurrier, pinioning him, while the raider struggled to reach the pistol at his belt, swearing a blue fog of obscenities.

"Help!" Charlie bawled. "Oh, my Lord — help!"

Suddenly he blinked in daylight. Sun streamed through a rent in the canvas. Above the linked figures towered the bulk of Corporal Slink, Barlow knife in hand. "What the hell?"

Still holding fiercely to Mad Jack Spurrier, Charlie tottered to his feet. Together the pair stood in the center of a ring of incredulous spectators. About the camp was the litter of an unsuccessful Confederate raid; crumpled gray bodies, a saber stuck in the trunk of an elm, a haversack from which spilled parched corn. Firing was still going on down by the river but here it was quiet, the deathly quiet after a pitched battle.

"Well, I'll be damned!" Major Cairns marveled. Biting a chunk from a plug of Wedding Cake, he nodded to Slink. "Corporal, peel that dentist or whatever he is off our friend Jack Spurrier, late of the C.S.A."

Freed, the raider tried to reassemble his torn clothing. One sleeve had come loose at the shoulder, there was a rent in the thigh of his pants, and in the scramble under the fallen tent he had lost a boot. "If that damned tent hadn't fallen down," the late Scourge of the Shenandoah shouted, "you'd never ketched me!"

Rapidly Charlie recovered. "It was my idea," he explained. "I used to catch rats that way with a little

41

box propped up by a peg. I pulled the string, and the box fell down on them. Well, this is the same thing. I was the bait, you see, and —"

"Where's the general?" Major Cairns looked about, frowning.

Charlie blanched. His stomach did a sickening prolapse. "General Zwick? Why — ah —"

"He was in there with you! Weren't you working on his teeth?"

"I — I —" Charlie's voice failed. He was about to confess he had killed the general in an excess of anesthesia but his vocal cords were strung too tight. All that emerged was a high-pitched squeak.

"Look!" While putting hastily summoned manacles on the dejected Spurrier, a pink-cheeked lieutenant stared wide-eyed at the collapsed tent. "Look there, major, sir!"

Under the canvas was a gentle excrescence. As they watched, it rose, swayed about. The excrescence spoke in German. Like a wave on a canvas sea the mound moved toward them; the canvas rippled. Charlie paled. General Zwick's ghost! A nightmare, that was what it was; a daytime nightmare! Hamlet probably felt the same way on seeing his father's ghost. Giddy, Charlie swayed and began to black out. No one noticed; all eyes were riveted on the apparition.

"*Mein Gott!*" The general's bald head appeared through the rent in the canvas. Blinking, he peered about. "What happen, *hein?* Something fall on me, I think!" Stepping cautiously out, he stared. "Why you all standing around loafing, eh? Isn't a war?"

Major Cairns stepped diffidently forward. "Sir, here is General Spurrier. He tried a raid on your headquarters but we —"

"Me!" His head clearing rapidly, Charlie quickly stepped forward to intercept the major. "*I* caught Spurrier, sir, when he dared to enter your tent! I hit him with the tent pole and —"

"Spurrier?" General Zwick prowled forward, eyeing the sullen captive, "Ah, so! Py jiminy! Now we got you, you *dumkopf!*" He drew himself up, scornful. "Spurrier, eh? Some Spurrier! A ragamuffin! He don't look like such a much now!" He gestured to Major Cairns. "Take him away and hold him for the provost marshal!"

"I caught him!" Charlie insisted. "You see, general —"

"Wait!" Wonderingly, General Zwick touched his jaw. "The tooth! *Ja*, the tooth!" He opened his mouth, explored with a stubby finger. "No pain! I don't hurt!"

"Yes, sir," Charlie agreed. "I did a good job on that, too, sir. I'm a very handy person."

The general clapped Charlie on the shoulder. "What was that stuff you giff me to drink, dentist? Very good! Make some more, eh?" Linking arms with Charlie Callaway, he shouted after Major Cairns and the guard detail. "This here is now my staff dentist, understand? Py jiminy, I give him brevet rank of lieutenant!"

"Thank you, sir," Charlie said. After all, what better place to hide from the Army than in the Army? Who would think to look for a three-time bounty jumper on the personal staff of General Peter Zwick? Anyway, the war was winding down; Spurrier's raid was probaly the last gasp of the dying Confederary, and Charlie

Callaway was no longer in danger of getting shot by anybody. It was a comforting thought.

In a benevolent autumn sun he swaggered about the camp, a privileged character, one-time civilian finery replaced by a melange of military items: a bright Zouave jacket won in a poker game, yellow-striped cavalry breeches, Wellington boots no longer needed by a Johnny Reb. He had his own tent next to the general's. With a vial of laudanum cadged from a passing Sanitary Commission train, he pulled more of General Zwick's pain-wracked teeth. He worked at the farrier's forge, fashioning for himself a new set of dental instruments — probes, lancets, and a levering pliers of his own design. He even made some progress on a jointed drill, a thing of rods and pulleys to be powered by the foot, though it still needed a better flexible cable than corps quartermaster stores could furnish.

His chief complaint was the loss of nearly a thousand dollars. Now that he had captured Mad Jack Spurrier and was somewhat of a celebrity, there was no further talk of his being a spy. By rights, then, they should return his money. But General Zwick only shrugged.

"A shame, *ja*," he agreed. "But that *dumkopf* Cairns turned it over to the corps finance officer — leastways what he didn't keep for himself — and no one knows now where it got to."

Privilege, even the assumed rank of lieutenant, bought no liquor at the sutler's wagon, no cigars, none of the appurtenances of comfortable life. Charlie was too proud to borrow from the junior officers who regarded him with admiration. While there was talk of a medal for his feat of capturing the Scourge of the Shenandoah, that would not buy anything, least of all the favors of the prostitutes who practiced their trade in the shacks and abandoned outbuildings surrounding the camp. Long balked by Lorna Bascomb's impregnable virginity, Charlie needed a woman but didn't have the price. They wouldn't even take his gold ring for a half hour or so of female company.

"It's real gold!" he protested. "See here!" He bit it, made a dent, but none of the Cyprians was interested.

"Cash only, mister," Madame Blanc, the entrepreneur, told him.

He shrugged and shambled off. Well, he would just have to use his native ingenuity. He brightened, remembering a trick Nathan Goodbody had described to him when he and the gambler were on the river. No, not a trick, really! Uncomfortable, he remembered the Old Gentleman at the pearly gates; he would not sin again. This was only a matter of knowing more about the behavior of ants and lice than anyone else.

Casually, he strolled through the camp, looking for a likely group to be edified. The atmosphere was convivial. Yesterday had been payday. In addition, General Grant had started a determined drive on Richmond and Cump Sherman had swung out from Chattanooga to girdle the Confederacy and take Atlanta. The war would soon be over; men would be going home to see their wives and children. Everyone felt happy and flush.

Chewing a blade of grass, Charlie squatted beside a bearded corporal plucking lice from his blanket.

"Nice day!"

The corporal, intent on his work, did not look up. "Guess so."

"Funny thing about lice," Charlie mused. "They're fast little creatures. Run about like anything. Faster 'n an ant, any day."

Some of the corporal's bunkmates, yawning and scratching in the sun, emerged from the dugout they had burrowed into the river bank.

"Oh, I don't know," the corporal said. "Ants is pretty fast, too!"

Charlie felt the old thrill; the fish had taken the bait.

"I'd put my money on a louse any day!" he insisted.

Interested, the company pressed around. There was much discussion, but the general agreement was that an ant could outrun a louse.

"Louses is dirty bugs, and bite like sin," a barrel-chested sergeant-major opined, "but they're slow, actual." Reaching out, he plucked a louse from the corporal's blanket and dropped it on the ground. "See?" The louse stumbled uncertainly about. "An ant is quick!"

"Well," Charlie said, judicially pursing his lips, "I'm not a betting man, but I'm might tempted to put some money on the proposition."

Bored with the backwaters of the war, they crowded close. "Mr. Callaway, how would you prove it?"

He caught sight of the tin pannikin of a mess kit being scrubbed in the river. Borrowing it so quickly the soldier did not have time to object, he laid it on the smoldering remnants of a cookfire. "Fair is fair. I'd say

— drop an ant and a louse on this hot tin and see which one gets off first."

The sergeant-major waved a greenback. "I've got five dollars says an ant is faster!"

The others looked cautiously at each other, began to fumble at sheafs of bills.

"I'll give odds!" Charlie said cheerfully. "My money's on the louse kingdom as fleeter of foot than winged Mercury himself!"

"Who the hell is Mercury?" someone wanted to know.

Warming to his pitch, Charlie ignored him. "Come on, you reckless gamblers! Five to one on the louse! What say?"

The proprietor of the mess pannikin looked sourly at him. "Where's *your* money, then?"

He had no money; all that was left was his ring. Holding it high in the sun so all could see the glitter, he said, "This ring is solid gold, given to me by a Hindu potentate for saving his life on a tiger hunt in Hyderabad, India. It's worth fifty dollars if it's worth a nickel! Here, sergeant; take a look at it."

"God, he talks funny!" someone muttered.

The sergeant-major hefted the ring tentatively. "But what's this little tit that sticks out, kind of?"

Hastily Charlie recovered the ring. "Well, you see that's just a kind of burr left when they made the ring. Gold does that sometimes, you know."

Satisfied, they dropped bills into a borrowed hat. Charlie counted. "Forty-seven, forty-eight — all in? Well, then, you're covered."

Someone held a louse gingerly between thumb and forefinger. The mess kit man probed in the sand and located a black ant with ferocious pincers.

"All right, then," Charlie instructed. "Drop 'em on the pan when I say go."

Watching him, they poised above the heated pannikin. "Go!"

The insects tinked on the hot pannikin and began to race about. The ant scurried to the edge of the pannikin, paused, uncertain, then skittered feverishly around the circumference in the manner of ants from time immemorial, looking for a way to escape. The louse lumbered directly to the edge and dropped to the ground.

"No contest!" Charlie announced. "I win!"

There was a chorus of protest. "That ant went twict as far as the damned louse, didn't he? And besides —"

Charlie shook the money out of the hat, pressed rumpled bills flat, stacked them neatly. "I can't be responsible for a crazy ant, can I?"

"But —"

"Thank you, gentlemen." Folding the bills and tucking the wad into the pocket of the Zouave jacket, he made to go, quickly. But they surrounded him. "Now wait a damned minute!"

"Fair is fair!" Charlie protested. He appealed to the sergeant-major. "What was the bet?"

The noncom scratched his beard, frowned, and finally spat a stream of tobacco juice into the dust. "He's right, you know! The bet was to see which animal got off the pan first. Mr. Callaway won fair and square."

"No hard feelings," Charlie said companionably. He peeled off ten dollars and threw it into the hat. "Spend that at the sutler's for a gallon of good bourbon whiskey, fellows; drinks are on me. Meanwhile, I hear General Zwick calling."

Leaving them open-mouthed, he hurried away. Casting an eye heavenward, he muttered, "It wasn't cheating! You can't call me on that! I've reformed!"

It was raining, a cold drizzling autumn Pennsylvania rain. For some reason known only to the brass, Zwick's brigade still was held on the line along the river. Bored soldiers played cards in moldy dugouts and tents while a pall of leaden smoke lay over the encampment. Charlie Callaway, still moderately flush with the money he had won, lay in bed on a dirty coverlet. Becky, one of Madame Blanc's less-soiled doves, lay alongside him in an upper bedroom of the rickety house that had been left by its farmer tenants after Gettysburg a year ago. He had thought Becky would relieve him but he found himself, even in her fevered embrace, thinking perversely of Lorna Bascomb — the dark serene beauty, her understanding of him and his difficult ways, the forgiveness he had finally strained to the breaking point. Becky, a slender girl with taffy braids, compact and short-coupled like a littly pony, nibbled briefly at his ear.

"Eh?"

"You have such long, delicate, fingers, Charlie. They know what to do to a woman."

"They're my fortune," he said, "and my curse."

Wrapped in the sheet, she squatted beside him, eyes solicitous. "What are you thinking, Charlie?"

"Nothing." With a sigh he laid down the sweet potato he had bought from the sutler.

"Come on, now!" She gave him a playful push. "I know better 'n that!" When he did not answer, only pillowed his chin on folded arms and gazed through the broken window, she became serious. "It's another girl you're thinking of!"

"Maybe."

"Ain't I enough for you, Charlie?"

"You're enough for any man, kitten. It's just that —"

She waited, patiently. In a retrospective mood, he went on.

"Life is funny."

"It is that, Charlie. Look at me, a whore, that never wanted more than to make a good home for my widowed mother!"

"My whole family were gamblers," he said. "Pa, Uncle Bill, Grandpa Callaway — I guess they were gamblers and race touts in England, in Wiltshire, where we sprung from. So what chance did I have? It's in my blood, like a taint. I fight it, but it always comes back on me."

Madame Blanc had another customer, but Becky shouted furiously down the stairs. "I ain't done yet!"

"Well, hurry!" Madame Blanc complained. "This ain't no place for romantic dallying!"

"It's the Devil's business," Charlie sighed. "I got into a lot of troubles because of it. I meant well, you see, but things always turned out wrong."

50

She ran a hand through his hair. "You're a good man, Charlie — I know that."

"And you're a good girl, Becky, in spite of being a whore. I bet you meant well too."

She began to cry. "I really did. But there was Ma, sick and old, and no money to buy coal or pay the grocery, so I had to do what I had to do. And then —"

"There were good times," he murmured, watching the raindrops bounce silvery off the rotting sill. "Nathan Goodbody and me — we worked the boats together, till he retired and went to live with his daughter in St. Louis." He thought with affection of the smoke-plumed paddlewheelers plying the Mississippi. The main saloon was always crowded with rich merchants, cotton factors, and land speculators anxious for a friendly game of poker to while away the time until Natchez, Vicksburg, or Memphis. He had been nineteen then, an awkward gambler, in danger of being shot, until Nathan Goodbody took him under his wing. Nathan, fiftyish, well-dressed and respectable-looking, taught Charlie Callaway everything he knew — the false cut, the cold deck, the careful trimming of cards to become "strippers," so-called line and scroll work shading parts of the design on the backs so they could be read. Even now Charlie had the ring Nathan gave him when they left the old *Robert J. Ward*. He was glad the soldiers had not caught on to the use of the sharp pin on the ring that permitted a knowledgeable gambler to press a barely perceptible "pimple" on a high card to identify it when he dealt.

"It all sounds so romantic!" Becky said, pressing her cheek against his bare chest. He had not realized he was reminiscing aloud about the fine old days.

"There was always a long bar," he went on, "with drinks for the high-stakers; brandy smashes, milk punches, eggnogs, French brandy. Oh, there was luxury! One captain had five hundred dollars melted to make the bell on his wheelhouse! And food! Becky, you can't imagine. Roast pheasant, oysters big as your hand, beef roasts crusty outside and pink in the middle, pork chops and pie for breakfast, pickles, preserves and sauces, fresh bread baked in the boat's ovens, pitchers of cream so thick it'd hardly pour out of the pitcher."

"Oh my, Charlie!"

"But I left it to be a dentist."

Becky was silent. Then she said in a soft voice, "For — her?"

He rolled over, sat on the edge of the bed, pulled on his pants and Zouave jacket, now damp and smelling of mingled sweat and face powder. "Yes — for her."

"You come back," she invited.

He looked at her, the small trim body, the pleasant face. Both of them were victims of bad luck. "I've about run out of money."

Half-naked, trailing the sheet about her, she came on small bare feet to reach up and kiss him. "Come any time. You don't need money with me, Charlie! You're a beautiful man!"

"Madame Blanc —"

"Screw the old bitch," Becky said.

In the rain he wandered back to the farrier's shop. In spite of the sergeant's grumpiness, Charlie's new status permitted him the run of the place. Now he worked at a bench on the foot-powered drill he was fashioning. He had rolled dice with a supply sergeant to get the brass rods and wire he needed, and already had the drill about half done. Stretching it out on the bench, basking in the heat from the forge where the farrier sergeant was making horseshoes, he examined his handiwork. Not bad so far; he was good with his hands, whether dealing cards or making dental tools. As he looked at the rods and pulleys and cords, however, a thought came to his mind. Here, nearly, was the makings of a good holdout! Many cardsharps had tried to make a workable holdout to supply a needed ace in a tight game, but none had been successful. The "bug" he still had was only so-so; someone might look under the table where its prongs held a card. A few gamblers were content with an inside pocket of a vest, but that was awkward. Absorbed, he laid out the pieces of the drill in different order. Borrowing a stub of pencil from the farrier, he started to sketch the ideal holdout.

"Eh?" He looked up at the interruption. The bearlike Corporal Slink stood near him, wrapped in a sodden blanket, rain dripping from his beard. "What was that?"

"I said," Slink repeated, "I and the fellers would like for you to join us in a little game of draw poker tonight in my dugout. You're a sporting man, ain't you? I heared what you did to those galoots in B Company with your little ants and louses game!"

Charlie replaced the pieces of the drill, ashamed of his thoughts. How could he have imagined such a thing! Death had brushed him with its wings; now he must think seriously of his soul. He dismissed the ideal holdout from his mind as a sordid bit of chicanery.

"No," he demurred, "I don't think so."

"Afeared?" Slink jeered, the cast in his eye rolling malevolently. "It's only penny ante!"

B Company had put Slink up to it, he guessed; they wanted their money back. Suddenly he remembered poor little Becky and the sad story of her mother, left without coal and groceries, and winter coming on. What better way to start his reform than to sit in on a game and make some money to send Becky Smike's poor old mother? Besides, the Army had taken his almost-a-thousand dollars and wouldn't give it back. Slink and B Company were the Army, too, weren't they? He was certainly entitled to get back as much from the Army as he could. Going to the sagging door of the shack, he looked up at the sky. A promising strip of blue had appeared, almost an omen. It's for a good cause, he thought. The old lady's a widow, and sick into the bargain. "You can't hardly hold that against me!" he argued. "Widows and orphans has got to be taken care of. It's in the Bible someplace!"

Slink had followed him, and peered curiously.

"Who you talkin' to?"

"Nobody you'd know," Charlie said. "I'll be there."

He was there, wearing his ring, after first roughing up his fingertips with a file to improve their sensitivity. As he suspected, the penny ante game did not last long.

After a dozen hands, the stakes gradually crept up. Charlie had only a few dollars and permitted the boobs to win most of the hands.

"This isn't my night," he mourned, while they looked crafty and anticipatory. "My deal, I guess!"

He was a little rusty but managed to mark three aces as he fanned the cards about the table.

"Better luck this time," Slink encouraged him. The sergeant-major puffed a stogie and grinned, looking at his cards. The man from whom Charlie had borrowed the mess tin pursed his lips and opened for two bits.

"That's a little steep, isn't it?" Charlie protested.

They pooh-poohed his concern.

"Well, all right," Charlie agreed. "I'm in, just to be neighborly."

The stakes grew steadily higher and he was nearly broke. In successive deals, however, he had pinpricked the other ace, and double-pricked all four kings. Now was the time to strike. Dealing in the guttering light of the candle, he was silent and tight-mouthed, marking in memory where the high cards went.

"Ain't mad, are you, Charlie?" Slink grinned.

"Well, I am running a little scared," he admitted. Scared? If they only knew the night he took that Richmond cotton planter for a thousand dollars and a genuine European "Jurgensen" gold watch with a diamond set in the stem!

"Open for five dollars," Slink said companionably.

Charlie called. "Cards?" he asked.

Slink drew two cards. The sergeant-major drew two. While he dealt, Charlie kept up a running patter. "Two

55

enough, Slink? Sure you don't need another card? How about you, sergeant?" When water dripped from the earthen roof of the dugout he wiped the cards quickly, riffled them, feeling for the aces, and finding two of them. "They're free, gentlemen, are the cards! Take all you want!"

Running off at the mouth that way, he sounded nervous. That was what he wanted them to think. Dealing to himself, he slipped the aces dextrously into his hand and sat back in his chair, looking disappointed.

"More bad luck, eh?"

"Not too good," Charlie sighed, gazing at two aces and a king kicker.

"Ten dollars," Slink announced, laying a crumpled greenback on the table.

The sergeant-major raised another ten, his beaming face wreathed in smoke from the stogie.

"Gentlemen," Charlie announced. "I'm almost broke. But you all know this solid gold ring. The sergeant can vouch for its worth." He slid the ring into the pool of light from the candle. "Twenty dollars I bet."

They were startled. "Twenty?" Slink asked. He looked again at his cards. "I ain't got but ten left."

One of the players who had dropped out whispered in his ear.

"All right," Slink muttered. "Split fifty-fifty, eh?"

The man reached into his pocket and took out a ten, handing it to Slink.

"You're called," Slink said. Beads of sweat stood out on his forehead and the cast in his eye swiveled alarmingly.

56

"Twenty, eh?" The sergeant-major looked thoughtful. "All right, then — I'll call."

They laid down their cards. Slink had a pair of kings with an ace kicker. The sergeant-major had a pair of queens. Casually Charlie spread out his two aces, along with a king, a seven, and a deuce.

"Looks like I win, gentlemen."

When he raked in the money and reclaimed his ring — the gamble of the ring had been audacious, with the telltale little prickle on the band, but Charlie had style — they were dazed, open-mouthed. Charlie put the ring back on, riffled the cards so they spun and leaped like joyful birds. "Whose deal is it?"

"I'm cleaned," Slink said in a hollow voice. The sergeant-major shook his head. "Too big a game for me!"

"Well, then," Charlie said, "guess I'll get a little sleep. I've got to pull another one of the general's teeth in the morning — if he's feeling good, that is."

When he left they were still sitting glumly around the table. The necktie party had backfired. The man who had loaned Slink ten dollars was demanding repayment. The sergeant cursed in a steady monotone. Outside, the night sky had cleared; it looked as if an Indian summer day would follow the rains.

Taking off his clothes and rolling himself in his blanket in the small tent he occupied next to the general's, Charlie felt prosperous. But he had not been asleep more than a few minutes when someone dragged him by the heels from the tent. In the moonlight Corporal Slink bulked huge and menacing; he carried a bayoneted musket. Beside him stood the barrel-chested sergeant-major. Together they shook him as a mastiff shakes a terrier.

"Where's our money, you damned cheat?"

He stared at them, menacing figures in the wan light of the moon. Except for the rasping snore of General Zwick and an occasional call from a sentry along the river, the camp was still.

"We want our money!" The sergeant held out the deck of Steamboat cards. "You marked these pasteboards! Where's that ring?" Slink tore it from his finger; Charlie yowled in pain.

"I thought so!" the sergeant muttered. "See, Slink — feel here! He puts little bumps on the cards so's he can tell what he's dealing. That's how he won."

Slink crawled into the tent and came out with Charlie's pants. "Here it is!" he crowed. "All our money, sarge!"

"Now listen —" Charlie begged.

"Shut up!" the sergeant snapped. "By God, I knew you was a slicker the minute I seen you!"

"What — what are you going to do?" Surely they would not risk General Zwick's wrath by harming his personal staff dentist!

For answer they pulled him away, protesting, heels dragging in the rain-wet grass. Charlie tried to scream but Slink clamped a paw over his mouth.

"Where to, sarge?" he asked.

"Deep in the woods, down by that old still. That way no one will hear him."

Ungently they bore him into the moonlit forest. Only faint and ghostly light penetrated the thick-layered leaves of elm, oak, and sycamore. There was a general smell of wetness and decay. Finally they stopped before an upended mashboiler riddled with bullet holes to stand him on his feet. His knees collapsed, and Slink jerked him upright again.

"Now listen," Charlie quavered, "Surely this can be straightened out before" — he swallowed hard — "before you do anything you'll — you'll be sorry for!"

The sergeant guffawed. "Hear that, Slink? Anything *we'll* be sorry for!" Chuckling, he took out a jackknife and trimmed branches from a sapling about the thickness of Charlie's wrist.

"We're gonna teach you a lesson," Slink told him patiently, as one instructs a backward child. "We're a-gonna beat you within an inch of your no-good worthless life for cheating dutiful Union soldiers that are already sacrificing their lives fighting for their country without being took in by rascals like you, Callaway!"

Far away he heard the faint call of a centry. It trembled and shimmered in the night, a thin wail. No one could hear him now even if he hollered his head off.

"Hold him, Slink!" the sergeant commanded.

Slink threw Charlie on the ground and sat on his head.

"Tear off his undershirt!"

The cloth ripped, came free.

"Now!" the sergeant said.

Face down, Charlie thought it sounded as if he were spitting on his hands. "No!" he moaned. Slink pushed his face further into the detritus of decaying leaves. His

59

mouth filled with dirt. In panic he wrenched his body, wriggled, and broke free of Slink's grasp. Slink reached for his ankles but Charlie jumped over him, desperate, while they both tried to recapture him. Panic-stricken, he dodged around trees while they pursued him, cursing.

"No!" he pleaded. "God damn it, fellows — listen a minute, will you? We can work this out!"

Too late he saw what Slink had snatched up. It was the musket, cocked and primed. Further argument was pointless. Slink had always wanted to shoot him; now he had his chance. Bounding like a deer over a fallen log, Charlie departed. In mid-trajectory the musket roared. He felt a blow on his back, near the shoulder. Heedless of pain, he skittered deeper into the wilderness of trees, tripping over wild-grape vines, splashing into and out of forest pools. Their voices, frustrated and angry, dwindled in the undergrowth behind him. Madly he plunged on, staggering, falling, picking himself up to run again. Who was that? What was that? Someone seemed to be going ahead of him, urging him forward, while he himself crawled and blundered through the muddy brush.

Come on, Charlie! You want them to catch you?

Blearily Charlie stared. His eyes were so smeared with sweat and mud that he could see nothing distinctly.

"Who's there?" he asked.

It's me.

At first he didn't place the voice. "I just don't understand! I mean well, God knows, but somehow or other I always seem to be running from something or someone! Lorna was right!"

The voice sounded annoyed. *No time for philosophy! Get up, man! Keep going!*

Now he knew the voice. It was the Old Gentleman, the one who had denied him entrance through the pearly gates.

"Why are you helping me? You didn't do me any good when I was up at your place!" Tired, he fell down again, slumping on muddy knees.

The voice had a thin shadow of a chuckle in it. *I don't know! Things get dull up here at times, and a man needs diversion. Maybe I just possibly saw a streak of good — just a pinch, mind you — in your miserable soul.* The voice seemed to drift ahead, and then return. *There's a road about a quarter of an earthly mile up there. I see it in the moonlight. Can you make it, Charlie Callaway? Maybe in the morning you can catch a ride on a farm wagon and light a shuck out of this Army country that don't agree so good with you.*

He could never make the road, he knew that. The quarter mile might as well be the length of the Great Wall of China. In fact, he found he could not even get on his feet again. Slowly he toppled into a thicket of berries, not even feeling the brambles.

"You go on," he told the Old Gentleman. "I'm sleepy. My back is wet, and it's probably blood. I'm going to rest here awhile."

CHAPTER
FOUR

He was in limbo, floating weightless in a void where there was no sound, no people — nothing. The feeling was not unpleasant, yet after a while it began to pall. Then, almost as a passenger in a balloon ascension at a county fair, he began to rise toward a diffuse light. At first it was only a pinkish glow; as he ascended it spread and grew until it filled his world. Fascinated, he watched as the glow changed to a new-minted golden mist, streaked with dark shadows.

"What's going on?" Charlie demanded.

He tried to move but a stab of pain lanced his shoulder. Wincing, he was content simply to lie flat — he seemed to be in bed — and watch the mist brighten into sunlight streaming through an open window. The dark shadows became a bureau, a table, pictures on a wall.

"Where am I?" he demanded.

Something moved at the corner of his vision. He rolled his head on the pillow to see a small boy in a wide-brimmed black hat scuttle away down a hall.

Cautiously Charlie propped himself on elbows, wincing again as the pain reasserted itself. Where the hell was he? What had happened? Uncomprehendingly

62

he stared at two crayon portraits on the wall — a bushy-bearded patriarch and a grim-mouthed grandmother in a close-fitting white bonnet. The room was filled with the aroma of bread baking, drifting in through the open door; below, he heard women chattering.

He swung bare legs over the edge of the bed and plucked unbelievingly at the flannel nightgown that encased him. Recollection at last restored his muddled mind. A moonlit night, Slink and that ugly sergeant-major, the headlong flight through the woods, then came the blast of Slink's musket and the heavy blow on his back. He pulled down the flannel, probing gingerly. His shoulder was swathed in a bulky bandage. Now who had done that? Even more important, as he remembered his dialogue with the Old Gentleman as he fell to the leaf-strewn earth, who had found him and brought him to this neat house of hooked rugs and baking bread?

When he stood up his head swam. With determination he lurched to the open window, holding on to chairs and the bureau, and peered out through the starched curtains.

The place seemed to be a farm. The buildings were a virginal white against green lawns and tilled fields. The milkhouse, the outhouse, the picket fence were all white, as were the trunks of the well-kept trees. Blinking in the sun, Charlie watched a group of girls clad in gingham dresses and the same kind of little white bonnets as the woman depicted in the portrait on the wall. They laughed and sported as they dug weeds from a vegetable patch beyond the snowy barn. The doors and the space under the eaves of the barn were decorated with cabalistic designs in red and yellow and blue. Some memory stirred in him; those queer designs meant something.

As Charlie puzzled, a ferretlike little boy in the black hat scurried to the girls. Conferring, he pointed to Charlie's window. Charlie stepped into the shelter of the curtains as the boy and a young girl hurried toward the house. Quickly he got into bed and pulled up the sheets.

He felt rather than saw them enter. Suddenly there was a cool hand on his brow. "Mister, you are awake?"

Slowly he pulled down the sheet. The woman was young, probably in her early twenties. The taffy-colored hair, braided in heavy strands, was neatly stowed under a white cap, and her eyes were a cornflower blue. She was not pretty — not beautiful, that is to say — but very wholesome and feminine.

"Yes," he agreed. "I — I am awake."

Handling him easily (she was good-sized) she raised him to examine the bandage. "*Ach*, good!" Sensing his wariness under her gentle touch, she spoke reassuringly, wiping hands on her spotless apron. "*Nu*, don't be afraid, mister! We protect you, we take care of you!"

Nose sharp and eyes small and intense, the small boy, his face making Charlie think of a dried apple, said, "He's a reb, then — ain't it, Emma?"

They thought he was a reb! Well, let them think so until he had evaluated the situation.

"But you don't need to worry," Emma assured him. "You're safe here, mister."

64

If he was safe as a reb in this refuge, then he would be a reb. "Yes," he said heavily. "An officer in A. P. Hill's Third Corps." Lorna said she always knew when he was telling a fib because he avoided her eyes. He resisted the habit. Anyway, they seemed rustic folk, and would hardly know that the Confederate general A. P. Hill and his Third Corps had not been in Pennsylvania since Gettysburg, over a year before. He was grateful he did not have to explain how he came to be left behind.

"You must be hungry. Can you eat, mister?"

Come to think of it, he *was* hungry.

"Peter," Emma said, "go now to the kitchen and bring Mr. — Mr. — ah —"

"Callaway," Charlie said. "Captain Charles Chaney Callaway, ma'am, of Chattanooga, Tennessee."

"Bring Captain Callaway a glass of milk and some of them molasses cookies on a tray. Wash your hands first, though. You are always so dirty!"

"I ain't neither!" Peter complained, but scuttled away. A disagreeable little boy, Charlie thought, who bears watching.

"No fever," Emma mused, putting a hand on his brow.

"I — I don't know what happened," Charlie said, perhaps more feebly than necessary. "How did I get here?"

"Papa found you near the road when he went into town with a load of cheeses and potatoes for the market."

"Papa?"

"My papa. Mr. Amos Stoltzfus." She pointed. "That's his picture over there. And Mama, though she passed over long ago." She dropped her eyes and smoothed her apron when she saw him stare at her. "We're Old Order Amish and don't take part in no wars nor nothing like that." Still uncomfortable under his gaze, she blurted, "You look *stroovlich*, you do!"

"*Stroovlich?*" That must be Dutch dialect, he thought.

"I forgot you are *anner Satt Leit!*" Then she giggled, putting a hand over her mouth. "The other kind, you are! Not like us. *Stroovlich* means — well, your hair is all mussed and your face is dirty!" She rose to pour water into a basin and pick up a comb. "Now, then!" Kneeling beside the bed, she bathed his face with the cloth; he winced, finding an egg-sized bump on his forehead. "Oops! Did I hurt you?"

A deep rumbling from the doorway, a bearlike sound, startled both of them. The massive man from the crayon portrait stood there, clearing his throat. Emma jumped to her feet.

"You feel better, sir?" Papa Stoltzfus asked. He was a stolid man in a long black coat, a broad-brimmed hat, and boots heavy with mud.

"Yes, sir — I guess I have you to thank for saving my life, sir."

"The girls and I was having a weeding frolic when Peter came to tell me he was awake," Emma explained. A braid fell from the starched cap and she hastily pushed it in place. "So I just come up, Papa, and —"

66

"There is more weeds," Papa said. "Better you should not waste time up here, Daughter!"

"Yes, Papa." Obediently Emma wrung out the cloth, put the comb back on the bureau. With a sidelong glance at Charlie Callaway she left the room.

"Your daughter is a very nice lady," Charlie observed.

Papa Stoltzfus nodded. "A little flibbertygidget at times, but a good female. She's plain, but Emma makes a good wife to some man that don't mind her being so old." He took off the hat and wiped the sweatband with a finger that seemed as big around as Charlie's wrist. "I cut out your bullet. It just kind of plowed along under the skin. In a couple days you'll be *rumsprining* around." With a nod of the massive gray head, he closed the door. A moment later Charlie heard the heavy boots clumping down the stairway.

Stroovlich, anner Satt Leit, rumsprining — Charlie shook his head. What queer people were these Pennsylvania Dutch! Still, all in all, they had saved his life and offered to hide him. More weary than he had realized, Charlie sagged back on the feather pillow and slept, slept for a long time, forgetting even the molasses cookies and milk he had been promised.

Unlike most Amish families, that of Amos Stoltzfus was small, Mama Stoltzfus having died young in childbirth. There was Papa, the daughter Emma, a younger daughter named Clara, and ten-year-old Peter. The farm was prosperous and thus far untouched by the war. Papa hired several young men to help with chores. All had their eye on the lissome pink-cheeked Clara, but she was promised to Cleon Zook; the marriage would take place in November when the crops were in.

"Your sister is very pretty," Charlie remarked to Emma. Convalescing, he sat in a chair near the window, eating the breakfast Emma had brought on a tray. Inclined to be thin, he was beginning to take on heft from the abundant fare; eggs, fried mush, headcheese, liverwurst, bread, apple butter, and *schnitz* — pie made from dried apples that was rich with honey and raisins. The air in the Stoltzfus house was always redolent of boiling ketchup, frying meat, and cinnamon buns in the oven. "I don't wonder that all the boys make eyes at her!"

Emma bustled about the room, smoothing his sheets, shaking pillows out the window. "*Ja*, she is pretty! I am the ugly duck of the family."

"You are not! Why, Emma, you are pretty too!"

She plumped the pillows back on the bed. "But an old maid I am! No one wants an old maid like me! So I cook and wash and make for Papa and the rest. That is my fate, captain."

In shirt and pants borrowed from Papa draped grotesquely on his frame, Charlie rose and teetered toward her. "Emma, don't talk like that! You're sweet and gentle and a looker. Some day soon you'll be married too!"

"No! It is too late. But — but you are nice to say so."

Charlie, shaking his head, wandered to the window. Outside, early fall colored the scene. The hired hands, under the supervision of Papa Stoltzfus, swarmed in the fields and about the barn. Tobacco was being racked up to dry, potatoes dug, corn cut and shucked, cornstalks shredded for fodder, and the silo filled. At the neat square-cut borders of the fields the trees were red and yellow and brown. The sun shone, the air was chilly, crisp, and laced with wood smoke. Too old! What an idea! Charlie took a deep breath of the invigorating air, thinking it good to be alive. Emma had smelled clean and wholesome, womanly. A trace of desire rose in him, quickly dispelled when Peter's small shrewd face appeared in the doorway.

"Emma says maybe you want to read." He handed Charlie a worn leather Bible and a dog-eared copy of *Selected Sermons* by Pastor Friedrich Volker. Charlie laid them on the bed.

"To tell the truth, Peter, I'm not much of a reader."

"You want a chaw of tobacco? I got some hid away."

"Your papa let you chew?"

"No. But he don't know."

Charlie drew out the deck of cards, all he had managed to salvage from his career as staff dentist to General Zwick. "You ever play with the pasteboards?"

Peter's gaze was disapproving but there was a glitter in the small close-set eyes. "The *Ordnung* says no card-playing!"

"The what?"

"The *Ordnung!* The rules. The Old Order rules!"

"I'll bet the *Ordnung* says no tobacco-chawing, either. Anyway, not by little kids."

"I ain't no little kid!"

"Well, anyway —" Charlie spread the cards on the quilt. "Take one."

"Why?"

"To see who deals! I'm going to teach you how to play Old Sledge."

With a glance at the open door, Peter scuttled onto the bed, squatting cross-legged like a small Buddha. "All right. But hurry. Papa and the hands will be coming in pretty soon for dinner."

The boy was a quick study. Charlie had all he could handle to stay ahead in the score. After a while, he demanded, "You sure you never played this game?"

Peter looked guilelessly at him and arranged his cards in a freckled fist. "*Nein!* But it's an easy game."

"Not *that* easy," Charlie grumbled.

After winning two more games Peter asked, "Don't people sometimes play cards for money?"

"Sometimes."

"Why don't *we* play for money?"

Charlie examined his hand. Hopeless! Was the little weasel dealing off the bottom? "I haven't got any money, you know that. I'm a penniless refugee from the terrible jaws of war."

"That's all right. You can owe me. I heard Papa say that when you were up and around he would pay you to help out with milking. We're short-handed, you know."

Warily Charlie felt the corners of the cards. Was the scoundrel marking them somehow?

"All right," he finally agreed. "Five cents a game."

He had thought the high stakes would discourage Peter. After all, when Charlie was a boy a penny was a lot of money. But Peter only grinned a gap-toothed grin and held out his paw. "Shake on it?"

"Shake," Charlie agreed.

Soon there were loud voices below, a creaking of the pump handle outside the kitchen door, burbling and gasping noises as men plunged faces and hands into the basin. Quickly Peter rose.

"I got to go!" Taking a pencil and a scrap of paper from his pocket, he scribbled. "That's four bits you owe me."

"You don't have to write it down," Charlie grumbled. "I won't forget!"

As fall wore on, the nights grew colder. In the mornings there would be a skim of ice on the pond where the ducks swam. Frost laced the windows, and Charlie was grateful for the thick feather mattress and coverlet. He sank in like a bug in a cocoon, sleeping soundly to arise feeling replenished and restored. As winter peeked around the corner, Charlie's wound healed, leaving a ridged scar across his back. Soon he was invited to work as one of the hands, milking cows, hanging up broad leaves of tobacco to dry, cranking the feed grinder, and shucking field corn with a hook fastened to a leather glove. The bearded young men were courteous but not particularly friendly; it was clear that Captain Callaway was *anner Satt Leit* — the other kind.

Wheeling sacks of potatoes in a barrow, he dumped them on the earthen floor of the cellar and wiped his brow. The work had begun to harden him, give him unaccustomed muscles, ones rarely found in a dentist — or, for that matter, a gambling man. Emma was busy tallying stores: crocks of pudding, sausages, dried beef, fragrant hams, glass jars filled with red beets, beans, corn, chow-chow, piccalilli. In the dimness of the cellar her face glowed with radiant pride.

"*Ach*, when I put up all these things I was wore out! Never did I want to see another bean, another red beet! But now —" She gestured proudly. "Don't they look nice?"

Perspiring, though the morning had the chill of frost in it, Charlie sat on the empty barrow, fanning himself with his hat. "You *should* be proud, Emma. I never saw anything in a grocery in Washington to compare with your cellar. Not even Cruchet, the caterer on the Avenue, has anything to compare with this!"

She wiped her hands on the spotless apron and came close, curious. "Caterer? What's that? And what avenue?"

"Washington. Pennsylvania Avenue."

"I never been no place but here!"

Reminiscing, he crossed his legs and leaned back against the stone wall of the cellar.

"There was so much going on all the time, like the Patent Office ball and the big *soirées* at Willard's and the National!" He closed his eyes, remembering, and spoke drowsily. "Dancing is all the rage. Women in crimson velvet and pink and green silk and white tarlatan — the polka and the lancers — champagne corks popping. There were the theaters — Grover's on Tenth, Ford's that held twenty-four hundred people. I saw *The Naiad Queen* at Grover's; it cost me seventy-five cents but it was worth it!"

"I thought you was from Tennessee, captain."

He cleared his throat hastily. "I — I was a lawyer. I had business in Washington sometimes."

She came close, kneeling at his feet. "Tell me more, captain! It — it sounds so fine!"

"On the sidewalk are all kinds of salesmen — soap, pills, hair dyes, everything! Grocers have pyramids of apples and oranges and pineapples out in front. Ice-cream dealers are in the shade with their wagons, and the Italians roast chestnuts in little charcoal stoves. Ah, there's color, excitement! Swords and sashes, plumed hats, Navy officers in gold braid, ladies with spring bonnets! They wore a lot of red last spring; it was the color of Garibaldi's shirt."

"Gari — Gari — ?"

"An Italian patriot everyone was in love with."

Her eyes shone. "I can see the ladies now, all dressed up!"

"There is even a street railway," he went on, "right down Pennsylvania Avenue. You can ride on the horsecars from one end to the other. They —"

As a shadow brushed across the doorway, he broke off. Emma scrambled to her feet, adjusting the neat white *kapp*. Young Peter stood in the doorway, black against the sun, pale face peering.

"What you two doing in here?"

"None of your business!" Charlie exclaimed. "Aren't you supposed to be picking apples?"

"I'm done."

"You were spying on us, that's what!" Emma cried.

"No, I wasn't," Peter denied. "Anyway, where's that three dollars you owe me, captain?"

Charlie pressed hands against the small of his aching back. "Don't worry. A gentleman always pays his gambling debts."

"I don't think you're no gentleman anyways!" Peter said balefully, and sauntered away munching on an apple.

"He thinks maybe you are a spy or something," Emma explained, putting a glass jar of cherries high on a shelf. "Imagine!" she laughed, wiping hands on her apron.

"So?"

"Oh, he is crazy sometimes, that Peter!" Then, loyally, she added. "But a good boy, really."

Peter would bear watching, Charlie thought. That little ruffian would sell his mother for a Barlow knife.

In late autumn they seemed a long way from the war. The tide of battle had receded from the fertile Pennsylvania lands of the Old Order. Only scattered troops remained in the vicinity, mostly conscripts who did not seem interested in the business of conflict. The Amish were indifferent to wordly affairs, but a passing tinware peddler left a copy of the *Washington Star* which Charlie read avidly. Sherman had captured Atlanta. Hood's army was threatening Nashville. Though the Rebs still held Mobile, Admiral Farragut had captured the forts defending the port and rendered it useless as a conduit for Confederate supplies. Washington, anticipating an early end to the hostilities, was in a holiday mood. *Pocahontas and the Webb Sisters* was playing at the National Theater. Mad Jack Spurrier, the Confederate raider, was confined in the Old Capitol prison. Miss Charlotte Cushman appeared as Lady Macbeth in a benefit which netted two thousand dollars for the Sanitary Commission. Charlie longed for the city lights. Yet here he was, exiled to a farm, of all places!

Still, there was some excitement at the Stoltzfus home. Clara, flaxen-haired and dainty — she took after her mother, Emma explained — was now to be married to Cleon Zook. Emma sewed madly on the wedding dress. "So small!" she marveled to Charlie, holding up the blue cotton dress with its white organdy kerchief and matching apron. The Old Order eschewed fripperies such as ribbons, laces, and fancy embroidery, but Emma's nimble fingers had made the dress modish in spite of the prohibitions. "I am like a cow. No way could I wear something like this!"

Pricking her finger with the needle, she jumped nervously and sucked the finger. "Now where has that Peter gone to? I need him to run upstairs and get me more thread."

Charlie, feeling uneasy, looked about. "I haven't seen him lately." It was true, Peter seemed to be absent a lot of late, not even wanting to play cards. By now Charlie owed him over five dollars.

"Well," Emma said, "he better tend to his chores or Papa will give him a hiding!"

The wedding day dawned clear. The sun rose early in a cloudless sky, birds sang, and ducks quacked happily on the pond. Charlie had never been invited to church, or even urged to attend evening prayer sessions in the parlor where Papa Stoltzfus read from the German

Bible; the Old Order were clannish in their religion. He stayed in his room and dozed after the hard labor of the day, awaking only briefly to hear them all below, singing lustily from their *Lieder Sammlingen* — the Amish songbook. Still, he was invited to attend the wedding, and Papa loaned him an extra *mutze* — the long black coat Amish men wore at such occasions.

Clean-scrubbed, no longer *stroovlich* or whatever it was Emma called him that first day, he shook hands with the bride, painfully conscious of the calluses on his hands. He hoped they had not permanently crippled his ability to deal the cards.

"My, you are lovely, Clara!" he said. "Cleon is a very lucky man to have you!"

She blushed prettily and thanked him.

"She is beautiful," Emma said, a note of longing in her voice.

When Clara had gone out to the yard where the altar had been erected in a bower of cornstalks and fall foliage, decorated with pumpkins and squashes to symbolize the Amish gratitude for a bountiful harvest, he whispered to Emma.

"Clara's not as pretty as you!"

There had been a sadness in her eyes but she brightened. "Captain, you are such a kidder!"

"I am not kidding." He pressed her hand, but she saw Papa looking and drew her hand away.

"I got to go now. The *Vorsinger* leads the singing, and I am the only alto."

At high noon, after singing and prayers for a happy wedded life, Clara and Cleon Zook were married by the bishop according to the *Ordnung*. The men set up tables on trestles and the wedding feast got under way. Charlie marveled at the quantity and variety of the food: fried chicken, roast duck, veal sliced and pickled, mahogany-colored sausages, cheeses, rabbit in a spicy gravy called *hassenpfeffer*. There were fried potatoes, clove-scented red beets, corn puddings, tapioca pudding, celery, applesauce, fresh-baked bread and biscuits, unsalted butter from the milkhouse, creamed peas and carrots, baked beans, and macaroni and cheese. For the table of the bride and groom there was a whole roast turkey, its skin brown and crackling. As was the custom, it was carved by a special official, the *schnitzler*. After all this there came monumental chocolate cakes, high-standing coconut cakes, flaky grape pies, juice-soaked cherry pies, and the Old Order shoofly pie, rich with butter and molasses and brown sugar.

Unobtrusively Charlie loosened his belt. Relegated to a side table with the rest of the hands, he felt relaxed and amiable and struck up a conversation with the solemn young man across from him — Hans Denlinger. Charlie had worked with Hans in the barn.

"Good food, *nu?*" He had gotten to talk almost like the Old Order himself.

"*Ja, gut!*"

He stared overhead at a hawk soaring on incandescent wings in the rays of the Indian summer sun. Atop the great white barn that was bursting with the fruits of the harvest, a covey of pigeons sat preening their wings and talking softly among themselves.

"Why don't you people use lightning rods? If lightning ever hit —"

"The *Ordnung* says no lightning rods. If lightning strikes, it is the Lord's will, *nein?* We do nothing against the Lord's will!"

"But —" Charlie was about to protest the argument when a kind of lightning did strike. First he was aware of Emma picking up her skirt, leaving the bride's table to hurry toward him. At the same moment he saw the mounted patrol of blue-clad cavalrymen at the gate. The noncom slid off his horse and sauntered toward the wedding party while the soldiers — no conscripts these, but hardbitten regulars — slouched in the saddle, waiting. The corporal ambled toward the wedding party like a blue-clad bear — Corporal Slink!

"Charlie!" Emma pulled at his sleeve. "Come quick!"

He looked around, feeling his heart thump against the walls of his chest. "Where?"

The milkhouse, reed-bordered stream running cool through its stony bulk, was nearby. Without answering Emma pulled him through the grape arbor, around the barn, and to the milkhouse.

"In here — *schnell!* Quick! The soldiers!"

When the door banged shut they were alone in the clabber-smelling dark. While they waited, hardly breathing, the stream burbled and murmured at their feet.

"*Lieber Gott!*" Emma breathed. "I hope they didn't see us." She clutched his hand. "Papa — Papa will have to tell them if they ask the question right. He — he will not lie. It is sinful to lie."

Charlie's mouth was dry and his heart pounded heavily. In that moment he had the awful feeling that he had been betrayed — sold by a small card-playing Judas with a sharp nose and eyes set too close together.

CHAPTER
FIVE

In darkness they waited. Emma squeezed Charlie's hand. "I am afraid!"

Afraid also, he said nothing. Why were they looking for him? The enlistment bonuses? Cheating at cards? Or did General Zwick want his staff dentist back?

There was no sound in the milkhouse except for the beating of their hearts and the trickle of spring water as it curled around the base of the milk jugs. From a distance they could hear the faint sound of voices, Papa's heavy basso against the querulous military voice, but could not make out the words.

"Do you think they saw you?" Emma asked.

Charlie pulled her closer. "I don't think so. Coming through the grape arbor and around the barn like we did, I don't think anyone knows where we went — yet."

Emma put her eye to a crack in the oaken door. "The soldier is talking to Papa." For a long moment she was silent; then she said, "Clara is bringing the soldier a piece of pie." When she straightened he could smell the clean smell of her, feel her plump animal warmth against the cool of the milkhouse. Suddenly, unexpectedly, she put her head against his breast.

"I don't want them to catch you, Charlie!" She wept.

Warming to the gesture, he finally pulled himself away to press his own eye to the crack. Good Lord! Was Slink turning his gaze toward the milkhouse?

"What is it, then?" Emma asked.

"'When in disgrace with fortune and men's eyes,'" he murmured, "'I all alone beweep my outcast state — '"

"It sounds like poetry," she whispered.

"It is. William Shakespeare. I am an unlucky person. He said it all for me."

"It's beautiful but I don't know for sure what it means."

He kissed her, chastely, on the brow. She drew back, then pressed closer. "Oh, Charlie!"

"But I like the way it ends," he said. "' . . . For thy sweet love remembered such wealth brings/That then I scorn to change my state with kings.'"

"*Ach*, it's beautiful!" She wept, blew her nose with a handkerchief.

The milkhouse seemed too warm. Charlie ran a finger around the tight collar of his linsey-woolsey shirt. Emma's ample breasts were pressed tight against his chest. Distressed, he bent again to the crack. His heart leaped; Corporal Slink and the patrol had mounted, waving farewell to Papa, who stood large and straight at the gate in his *mutze*.

"They're leaving!" he cried. In dim light through the cracks in the door he put his arms about Emma, lifting her high although with some difficulty; she had heft to her. "Emma, they're gone!"

She kissed his cheek. "Charlie, I prayed! *Unser Gott* answered my prayer! You are saved!" She wanted to kneel in thanksgiving but Charlie held her tight.

"Oh, Charlie!" she said, over and over. "My goodness! You hold me so I can't breathe yet!"

The escape from capture exulted him. Emma excited him also. He kissed her fair neck, nibbled her ear. "'O! the world hath not a sweeter creature; she' — my Emma, that is — 'might lie by an emperor's side and command him tasks.'"

Frightened by his passion, she protested. "I do not lay by anyone's side, Charlie! I am a good girl!"

"Good? Emma, you're the best! Do you know — I think I love you!"

When the door opened his lips were pressed tight against hers. Bathed in sunlight, they stood locked together. Emma gave a frightened gasp; Charlie slowly turned his head. It was no use relaxing his embrace. He was caught in the rays of the sun as a fly is preserved in amber.

"Here they are, Papa!" Peter's childish treble was tinged with satisfaction. "I told you they went in here."

Papa's face was somber. "So! In here you make love, eh?"

Charlie let her go, straightened rumpled clothing. "It's not what you think, sir! I mean —"

The stony gaze reminded Charlie of an Old Testament prophet confronting Babylonians. Behind Papa some of the wedding party peered in, shocked.

"If it is not what I think, then what is it?" Papa rumbled.

Without much success Charlie fumbled for words. "Don't blame her! It was my fault. I — I took advantage of her. You see, I was so happy that I —"

"Emma!"

Slowly she came forward, head down.

"Go now to your room!"

With an agonized glance at Charlie Emma fled down the graveled path, the wedding guests drawing aside as if she were unclean.

Papa's broad-brimmed hat and the black *mutze* were the habiliments of a hanging judge. Well, Charlie had erred; he deserved his judgment. And Emma, poor Emma! In this strict society she would be judged a fallen woman. Now no man would want such a libertine.

"Listen," he pleaded, without much hope. "Please listen! I — I —"

"The soldiers were looking for a deserter," Papa said heavily. "A dentist and a cardsharper. They were not looking for you. Anyway, they are gone, Captain Chaney. And you will be gone, too, from my house and my lands before the sun goes down. *Verstehen Sie?*"

Charlie sighed. "I understand. But I thank you for the kindness you and your — your household showed me in time of distress. I'm sorry it turned out this way." Charlie walked down the graveled path toward the house. The wedding guests muttered among themselves, drew, aside. Things had gone abysmally wrong. Worse, he had hurt Emma Stoltzfus, given her reputation a mortal wound. God, what a fool he was!

In the bedroom he put a pair of socks and another shirt in an empty grain sack, along with the dog-eared deck of cards. "I meant well," he said defensively to the ceiling. "You can't blame me for everything! I was trying!" He broke off when Peter's shrewd face appeared at the doorway.

"You little sneak! Why did you tell them we were in the milkhouse?"

"That's where you were, ain't it?"

Charlie could not refute such logic.

"When you going to pay me the eleven dollars you owe me?"

Charlie tied a knot in the neck of the feedsack, threw it over his shoulder. The wedding party had ended; the sun was low in the west behind a burnt-umber haze.

"There's no getting blood out of a turnip!" In fact, he had over ten dollars saved; it was wrapped in one of the socks.

"I don't know about turnips," Peter countered, "but I know Papa gave you money, and there's no place around here to spend it. Pay up!"

"You go to hell!" Charlie made for the door, pushing the little imp aside.

"You ain't no reb!" Peter cried.

In the doorway, Charlie paused. "What did you say?"

Peter stood his ground. "You ain't no reb! I know who you are. You cheated me enough at cards so I know. You sound just like the man the soldiers was looking for. A deserter and a cardsharper. Maybe a dentist, too. Didn't you look at Emma's tooth the other day when she said it pained her?"

Charlie closed the door quickly, put down the sack. "Hush your mouth! You want everyone to hear?"

Peter's small eyes glittered. "You think I'm some kind of a rube just because I live on a farm? I know where to get hold of that corporal, and I'll tell on you unless you —"

Charlie put a hand over Peter's mouth. Peter bit him.

"All right!" Charlie said hastily. "All *right!* Just shut up your caterwauling!" Opening the sack, he took out the sock. "Here! Five dollars! It's all I've got!"

"Let me see!"

Charlie groaned, handed him the sock.

"Ten dollars, and some pennies! You owe me eleven dollars and —"

"I know," Charlie sighed. "Take it all! I'll starve to death on the road, or freeze in somebody's woods, but I guess you don't care!"

Silently he went down the back stairs. The house was quiet; no preparations were being made for the evening meal. The atmosphere was sad; a pall lay over the household. He was glad he encountered no one.

Outside, the yard was steeped in dusk. He shivered as a cold wind touched him. Dry brown leaves drifted into the debris of the wedding feast. The guests were gone. For a moment he stood in the dust of the road and looked back at the Stoltzfus place; the white house, ghostly in the twilight with no lights behind the windows, the huge barn with its *hexerei* designs, the pond where the last wan rays of the sun reflected. "When in disgrace with fortune and men's eyes —"

Pulling the meager shirt tightly around his chest, he stepped out into the road and did not look back.

In late autumn Charlie walked a lot. Keeping an eye out for pursuers who might be following him for a variety of misunderstandings, he walked, begged rides on passing farm wagons, and walked some more. In Indian summer he sat on a milestone near Shippensburg and took off worn boots, wiggling his toes through the holey socks. Lorna. Where was Lorna now, what was sweet Lorna doing?

Mount Dallas, Bedford, Cannonsburg — wearily he trudged through Pennsylvania, coming at last to the National Road, the westbound thoroughfare. At Bellaire he crossed the Ohio River on the ferry and found a day's work helping out at a flour mill. In Zanesville he pumped a bellows at a blacksmith's shop and got a dollar, twenty cents of which went for a new sweet potato.

He arrived in Columbus, Ohio, as the Franklin County fair began. Charlie walked the grounds, watched the cattle judging, enjoyed the mighty farm horses straining to pull heavy loads on wooden sledges, and marveled at Professor Fogarty's red, white, and blue hot-air balloon as it took passengers up for two bits apiece. The crisp air was redolent of grilling sausages, candy apples, buttered popcorn, and crusty chicken legs. Charlie was tempted to spend his last dime on a piece of hot chicken at a stand but suddenly changed his mind. These ruddy simple people, these horny-handed sons of toil, might like to wager some of

86

their undoubted profits from a bountiful harvest on three-card monte. After all, they deserved a good time, didn't they, after all their hard work? He spent the dime on a fresh pack, of playing cards at a stand that was selling knickknacks and found a secluded spot behind a clump of sumac at the edge of the midway. By mysterious gestures he attracted two or three bucolic gentlemen and riffled the deck.

"You folks ever try three-card monte?"

Good-humored, they shook their heads.

"It's a very easy game." He looked warily around; there were constables patrolling the grounds who would probably look with disfavor on a gambling game at such a wholesome event. "A lot of money can be made by gentlemen such as yourselves if you have a sharp eye." He dealt out the cards on a tree stump. "You see, the ace of hearts here is called the baby."

"The baby," they repeated obediently. I've got two live ones, Charlie decided.

"Now the baby is the winning card." Shuffling the deck again, he laid three cards face down on the stump, observing with satisfaction that the two farmers had noticed the baby had one corner slightly bent. He had, of course, slightly bent the corner of the deuce of clubs also; the baby, the ace of hearts, was now safely hidden in the pack he held in his hands. He started the remembered spiel.

"Now, gentlemen, if you have that keen eye, the observant eye, you are about to make a mint of money." He made a series of lightning shifts of the cards, flipping them about fast but not too fast, watching the way the greedy stares followed the card with the slightly bent corner.

"You, sir!" He addressed the first man, a gaunt ancient with a beard like a billy goat's. "You sir! I will give you ten to one odds that you can't pick out the baby!"

The farmer pulled at the beard. "If I bet you a dollar —"

"Then I'll give you *ten* dollars!"

Billy Goat Beard conferred with his companion, a small wiry man with lips pursed like a shriveled apple. They nodded in unison.

"Put down your dollar then, sir." Charlie shuffled the cards again. "I'm making it too easy. Now take another look. Think you can still find the baby, that precious ace of hearts?"

"Sure," the little man grumbled. "When does the dinged game start?"

"The ace of hearts is the winning card! Watch it close!" By this time other farmers had gathered, curious. "It is very plain and simple but you can't always tell! I warn you, gentlemen, this is my regular trade, to move my hands quicker than your eyes! But fair is fair! Which one, sir, is the ace of hearts? Quick, now!"

Smirking, the old farmer reached for the card with the slightly bent corner, picked it, threw it face up on the stump. "There she is! Right there! The ace of — of —" He looked shocked. "That ain't the ace of hearts! That's the damned two of clubs!"

Charlie swept up the dollar. "So it is! Well, you can't win all the time!"

The two withdrew, muttering, and talked in low tones. Others crowded around, however. "How does this game go, mister?" a strapping young farmer asked. His wife tugged at his sleeve but he pushed her away. "I know what I'm doin', Katy!"

Charlie went through his spiel. "Takes a quick eye, young man! But I'll give you ten dollars for one if you spot the lucky baby, the ace of hearts!" He palmed the ace from the deck, gave it a quick twist to replenish the bent corner, and laid the three cards face down.

"Put in your dollar, then." He went into his pitch. "Remember the ace of hearts is the winning card, remember, young sir! Watch it close! Follow it with your eye as I shuffle! A big risk, true, but a magnificent reward if you guess the location of that precious ace! I always have two chances to your one but I give ten to one odds, so you're way ahead of a poor businessman like me!"

He heard the covert remark of Billy Goat Beard. "Some business, I must say!"

Feeling magic return to his long-unaccustomed fingers, he riffled the deck, palmed the ace of hearts, replaced it with the seven of diamonds this time, corner suitably bent. Disheartened apparently, the first two farmers had drifted away. Charlie didn't care; now there were plenty of other suckers. With a flourish he spread out the three cards again, face down. "Take your pick, friend! Which one is the baby, the card that makes you ten dollars richer, *plus* your original investment!"

Joyfully the young man picked up a card, stared at it. "That ain't it!" he said, shocked.

Charlie flicked the card from the farmer's fingers. "Why, so it's not!" He held up the card. "Folks, it's the seven of diamonds."

"Wait a minute!" the farmer protested, but Charlie had already scooped up the dollar.

"Who wants to try next, folks? A game of skill and perception!"

"James!" the young wife complained. "You've been swindled!"

Charlie moved in hastily. "No swindle, ma'am! I'm licensed by the fair board. If you have any complaints, send them to the governor at the state house."

He had collected eleven dollars when he saw the first pair of rubes approaching with a constable. "Game closed, friends!" he announced, dropping the cards into his pocket and dodging around the sumac bush. Running, he fell over a tent rope and bruised his shins. The constable pursued, followed by the two old farmers, who made noises like a pack of hounds baying a treed coon. Staggering up, he ran again, looking back over his shoulder, and knocked over a stand that was selling lemonade. He felt the sticky liquid drench his shirt. The lemonade man, shaking his fist, joined in the pursuit. Charlie dodged into the crowd on the midway and managed to lose himself. His pursuers cast back and forth along the edge of the crowd, looking for him, but he pressed close to a small family group and hunched over to appear shorter.

"Mama?" a small girl inquired.

"Yes, dear."

"Why is that man all wet in front?"

Charlie bolted for the merry-go-round and made one turn before stepping off again. Lungs laboring, heart pounding, he climbed into a pen with a ewe and a flock of lambs. Taking off his shirt, he hung it over the rail to dry and sank down among the bleating lambs. After a while the shirt had pretty well dried. He turned it inside out to present a different appearance, smeared dirt on his face to look like a roustabout, and climbed over the rail. He could not see his pursuers, and he had eleven dollars in his pocket. Sauntering about in the autumn sunshine, he felt pleased. Eleven dollars! For further disguise he bought a straw hat and a candy apple. Noticing the red, white, and blue bulk of the hot-air balloon, he walked over that way, chewing.

"Young man!"

Frozen, he halted.

"I need a helper," Professor Fogarty said. Fogarty was a big-bellied man in a plug hat and long nankeen coat, the map of Ireland written on his pug-nosed face. He added something unprintable. "I got a full load, and that bastard nephew of mine has got hisself so drunk he can't stand up!"

"I don't need a job," Charlie said, "but thank you very much."

The passengers in the basket were growing annoyed. "When do we go up, professor?"

"There ain't anything to it!" Professor Fogarty implored. "All you got to do is let the rope out on this winch, and then crank her down when I yell."

"Sorry," Charlie said, "but —"

From a corner of his eyes he saw a constable, peering this way and that, twirling a mace. The constable looked mean.

"I've reconsidered," Charlie decided. "Show me how it works." He lurked behind the big winch while Professor Fogarty explained.

"Give you a dollar for the rest of the day. Maybe by morning I can sober Delbert up."

Three-card monte made money faster, but he could hardly object, especially if he wanted to stay out of the Franklin County jail.

"Agreed," Charlie said.

Up went the balloon, Professor Fogarty manipulating ballast while maintaining a running commentary on the beauties of central Ohio as seen from a balloon. For two bits he gave the passengers a fifteen-minute ride — a bargain, Charlie thought. Anyway, the longer the balloon stayed aloft the less painful winching-down he had to do. After a while he became bored. Fifteen minutes! That was enough time to make some more money. Getting out his cards, he shuffled them and spread out three cards on a large packing case that had apparently contained balloon gear.

"A little game of skill, folks! Come try your luck! Ten to one odds if you guess which is the baby, the lucky ace of hearts!"

He managed to collect one or two dollars during each balloon flight, all the time watching cautiously for constables from behind the winch and enticing customers with welcoming jerks of his head and a riffle of the deck. These were good civilized people, he thought, accepting the loss of a dollar with equanimity — Germans apparently, used to authority, not questioning him or demanding to see the other two cards. He liked Columbus. A man could go far here. A man could —

Aware of distant shouting, he broke off in alarm. "Game's closed!" he announced, picking up the cards and handing an astonished teamster his dollar. "Sorry, sir. Time's run out. State law, you know." He ran back to the winch. From a height of a hundred feet Professor Fogarty leaned over the edge of the wicker basket, very choleric.

"God damn it, you deef? Pull us down, drat it! Quick, you dunderhead!"

In panic Charlie grabbed for the winch crank and missed it. Sprawling over the winch, he knocked the ratchet loose and the rope started to run out. The crank, still in its socket, spun madly, giving him a rap across the knuckles that he thought had broken his hand, his dealing hand. He tried to grab the spinning handle but it spun in a dizzy arc that looked like a shiny pie plate while the rope sizzled off the drum.

"Oh, God!" Licking his bruised hand, he saw the looped end of the rope break and fly off the drum. For a moment the frayed rope dangled like an Indian snake-charmer's cobra before his hypnotized gaze. Then it drifted into the air, swinging in the breeze. He made a wild grab for it but missed. The balloon soared higher and higher; Professor Fogarty's Hibernian wails grew fainter and fainter. Prudently Charlie dodged around a tent that housed a two-headed calf — "Ten

Cents to See the Monstrosity of the Century" — and joined the crowd gaping at the rapidly disappearing balloon, now somewhere over the Scioto River.

A gray-haired lady in a bonnet pulled at his sleeve. "What happened, mister?"

Charlie shook his head, spoke sadly. "Guess the rope busted, ma'am."

She was shocked. "Oh, my! What will happen to those poor people, then?"

"I don't know," Charlie admitted. He surely didn't.

As penance for his dereliction of duty he gave a dollar to a man collecting funds for orphans of Ohio soldiers killed in the war, after which he left the Franklin County fairgrounds with great speed. That night, flush, he took a room in the Farmers' and Drovers' Hotel on Third Street and treated himself to a supper of Lake Erie whitefish, browned crisp and succulent, along with all the trimmings. It was his first decent meal since leaving the Stoltzfus farm. But his stomach was unaccustomed to rich food, and that night he had bad dreams.

Charlie! Charlie Callaway!

It was the Old Gentleman. Terrified, Charlie sat up in bed, or seemed to remember in the morning that he did, trying to wrap his naked body in the sheet. He had finally had a chance to do his laundry, and his drawers were drying on the brass rail at the foot of the bed.

Charlie, I say!

"Yes, sir!"

I declare — I get busy someplace and you're smack dab into trouble again! Why I bother with you, I don't know!

94

"I can explain —"

The Old Gentleman fondled a lightning bolt. Charlie cowered.

"Please don't throw that thing at me! I meant well! I always do! It was just that —"

Just that! Just that! the Old Gentleman mimicked him. *It's just that you're worthless as a — a —* Words failed his inquisitor. *What I want to say I dassn't because it ain't fitting for these ivory halls up here!* Shaking his grizzled head, he spat into a golden cuspidor. *Those frostbit folks in that balloon got caught in an updraft and came nigh up here to me! I had to let air out of Professor Fogarty's balloon to keep them from trespassing on holy ground!*

"I didn't mean any harm! You see, I needed the money." A thought came to him. "I figured I'd travel out to San Francisco on the cars and see my beloved Lorna! That's all I wanted — just enough money to pay my way. What's wrong with that?"

The Old Gentleman hefted the lightning bolt, weighed it judicially. *You telling the truth?*

"As God is my witness!"

We have ways of finding out, you know. We have a special angel up here who specializes in getting confessions from people who fib their way in! I can send him down and —

"No, no! That isn't necessary! It's the truth!"

The Old Gentleman sighed. *I don't know if you're worth my trouble, Charlie Callaway! I thought I saw a speck of good in you amidst all that double-dealing and chicanery, but now I figure I been swindled, just like you swindled all those other folks!* He raised his arm, balancing the jagged lightning bolt.

"No!" Charlie implored. "Not that!" Wrapped in the sheet, he fell off the bed. "No! Please! Help!"

Someone pounded on the door. "What's going on in there? Open up!"

Dazed, Charlie sat up. He was cold and sweaty. His stomach churned. Silvery and chill, a shaft of moonlight shone through the curtains at the window; the dingy lace stirred in the night wind. Shivering, he tottered to his feet and opened the door. The proprietor of the Farmers' and Drovers' Hotel glowered at him.

"What the hell's the matter with you, mister! Caterwauling like that in the middle of the night! I got a good mind to throw you out into the street — annoying everyone so!"

Up and down the corridor men with nightcaps looked out, ladies with curlpapers stared. They were indignant.

"I'm sorry," Charlie said. "Ah — you see, I have these fits. A rare medical phenomenon, the doctor says. Come on me without warning. Oh, how I suffer! But I try to bear up under this terrible burden. I'm truly sorry I annoyed anyone, and I apologize."

"Well —" The proprietor was uncertain. But an old lady said, "Poor man!" and a reverend-looking gentleman in a nightshirt offered to pray for Charlie.

"Thank you, preacher," Charlie said, trying to look pale and wan, which was no great effort after his conversation with the Old Gentleman. "But with the Lord's help, I think I'll be all right now."

96

He closed the door and Went back to bed. Looking upward, he said in a muffled whisper, "I truly mean it, sir! From now on I intend to do nothing but good works. You'll see." Exhausted, he slept, and did not wake until the sun streamed through the window.

CHAPTER
SIX

Indian summer turned into late November with snow
flurries and brawling winds. Forswearing chicanery,
Charlie got a job as swamper on a freight wagon
hauling dishes, chamberpots, and china figurines from
Ohio kilns to the merchants of St. Louis. It was hard
work and his once-dextrous fingers became knobbly
and callused. Still, it got him out of Columbus, where
he understood that Professor Fogarty was looking for
him with a warrant. General Sherman had left behind
a ruined Atlanta and started on a victorious march
toward the sea, three hundred miles distant, laying
waste to the South's last stronghold and encircling
Lee's ragtag army. The war was nearly over and when
they had time the military authorities would probably
start looking for Charlie Callaway. The West — that was
the place! Gold fields, plains black with buffalo,
sloe-eyed Indian maidens! Unloading crates along the
St. Louis levee for steamboat shipment up the broad
Mississippi, he felt a twinge of conscience. No
sloe-eyed Indian maidens — he would remain true to
Lorna Bascomb! She would be proud to see him now,
hard-working and responsible, a model citizen. Hard

work, he told himself, was redeeming, and he was beginning to feel redeemed.

St. Louis was full of Germans. He found useful the smattering of the language he had picked up in the Stoltzfus household. Although the outdoor beer gardens were now closed, there was always great merriment and good fellowship at Uhrig's and Scheider's. There were several breweries and beer was cheap, with excellent free lunch of hard-boiled eggs, fat sausages called *blutwurst* and *knackwurst* and *bratwurst*, platters of sliced ham and *bierkase*. For a nickel glass of beer a hard-working man could fill his belly if he waited till the bartender was too busy to watch the free lunch counter.

As soon as he could, he started to look for his old mentor, Nathan Goodbody. Charlie owed a great debt to Nathan. He had not the least idea where the old man lived, but made a lot of inquiries. On a day off he wandered through the huge St. James Market, talked to tanners, mechanics, masons, carpenters, saddlers, roustabouts from the riverboats, big-chested glass-blowers, avoiding only policemen. St. Louis was a lively city, streets filled with drays, carriages, merchants bawling their wares in the winter sunshine. The "street Arabs" decried by the *Post-Dispatch* were children who darted like swallows through the crowds; bootblacks, newsboys, children selling matches, pins, needles, combs, fruit, flowers. In the slums around Lucas Avenue and O'Fallon Street was an area called the Kerry Patch where young criminals stole, picked pockets, and snatched purses; they lived in caves along the levee. Charlie felt a hand inside his hip pocket and quickly caught a slender wrist. A small girl in rags, eyes wide with fear, stared back at him.

"Why, you little guttersnipe —" Charlie started, but she twisted quickly away and ran for cover into a passing parade. He lit a cigar and leaned against a lamp post, watching the parade. Everybody loved a parade.

First came a severe-looking lady banging a drum. Following her were two more ladies stretching between them a hand-painted sign; in ragged black letters it said, "Votes for Women, Now!" While lounging spectators jeered, the ladies, in columns of four, bore steadily toward Forest Park, just west of the center of the city. As they marched they sang, disregarding the jeers and catcalls of the men who lined the board walkways.

We are St. Louis females, a thousand strong!
We fight for our rights as we march along!
No man can deny us; you men, just you try us!
It is time right now to right this ancient wrong!

The verse didn't scan, Charlie thought, but was certainly loud and determined. Some of the women were old alligators but many were young, fresh-faced, and attractive. Some wore dowdy clothes, others were in Parisian millinery. Suffragists, they were called. The *Post-Dispatch* had run an editorial condemning them for abandoning the hearth and their children for mannish ways.

For December it was warm. The sun shone on the river, the sky was filled with fleecy clouds like grazing lambs, and Charlie had money to jingle in his pocket.

Humming the catchy tune the suffragists had sung, Charlie followed the parade.

Forest Park was a large one, over a thousand acres in the middle of St. Louis. Now, in almost-winter, the grass was sere and brown, chestnuts, elms, redbuds, and post-oaks spare and leafless, the duck pond a glaze of ice. Smoking his stogie, he sat on a wooden bench listening to a lady orator convinced of her cause. Most of the jeering idlers had abandoned the parade. Now there was only a small gathering; old men taking the sun, nursemaids with charges in perambulators, children throwing a ball while doting mamas watched and knitted.

"Why do men decry the intelligence of the women who gave them birth? Why do men deny the vote to the very females who could steer this mighty nation on a safer course, avoiding war and violence, with a gentler hand on the wheel of the ship of state?"

Well put, Charlie thought. He was not swayed by the argument, but the buxom young lady with the ginger-colored hair tucked under a feathered bonnet was a skillful orator — or oratress? He sucked on the stub of the stogie and listened.

"I hardly need remind you that the early movers and shakers of our cause were remarkable females like Elizabeth Cady Stanton and Lucretia Mott, who as early as 1848 spoke out not only for the rights of women but for the rights of Negro slaves, anticipating our own President Abraham Lincoln! These women, unlike our male politicians, foresaw a great and bloody conflict unless the Negroes were freed!" The young lady's hat fell off as she declaimed with an uplifted arm,

101

and hastily she put it back in place, awry. "And I tell you arrogant men that there will be another great war unless you listen to us ladies and give us the vote which is our birthright!"

There was a scattering of applause, mostly from women, and a few languid boos from some old men who were playing checkers on an upturned box. As the meeting dispersed, Charlie sauntered away. Where the hell was Nathan Goodbody? He had prowled the city, all the way from the levee to the mansions of the Rive des Pères with its fine view of the city and the river. No one had heard of Nathan Goodbody, and time was getting short.

Along Fourth Street, near the levee, he paused before a ferret-faced man dealing monte. Watching with professional interest, he decided that the dealer was a third-rate performer, without Charlie's line of patter and quickness with the pasteboards. Still, it was interesting to watch the fox among the chickens, fleecing the farm boys fresh off the turnip wagon, the fat burghers with gold watch chains and flowered vests, the innocent-faced soldiers back downriver on leave from fighting the Sioux Indians up on the Missouri. A sudden thought came to him. Perhaps this man knew the Prince of Gamblers. Sidling up, he spoke from the corner of his mouth.

"You know Nathan Goodbody?"

The dealer did not look at him, only riffled the cards. "What you want with me, then?"

"Information."

"You police? A detective?"

"Hell, no! I deal a better game of monte than you do! I'm looking for an old friend — Nathan Goodbody. He and I ran a crooked game on the old *Robert J. Ward*, up from New Orleans."

The little man saw a policeman approaching, idly swinging a mace. Quickly he dropped his cards into a pocket, collapsed the folding table on which he had been dealing. "Try a little green cottage behind St. James Market!" he called back as he dodged into an alleyway.

It would be good to see Nathan again! With newly found integrity Charlie strolled past the approaching policeman, nodding pleasantly and saying, "Good afternoon, officer."

With little difficulty he found the small cottage, but his way was barred by an unfriendly bulldog which growled at him from the neat front porch. "Nathan!" he called in irritation. "Come get this damned dog!"

Lace curtains stirred, and the front door opened. A wizened figure in a shawl and carpet slippers shuffled out on the porch, leaning on a cane. "Tige! Come here!" With a final snarl, Tige trotted up on the porch and sat.

"Who the hell are you?"

"Nathan, it's me! Charlie Callaway!"

"Charlie!" The old man stared. "Charlie Callaway! By George, it is! Come in, come in!"

They sat together in the small parlor, Nathan pouring tea from a flowered porcelain pot. Charlie eyed the beverage with distaste. "Come on, Nathan! Haven't you got anything stronger?"

"I don't drink anymore, Charlie. I've took the pledge. There ain't a drop of spirits in this house. That's a promise I made to the Lord."

Charlie shifted uncomfortably, noticing the plush-covered Bible on the marble-topped table. Still, he was unconvinced.

"You — Nathan Goodbody — turned holy? The only time I ever heard you mention the Lord was when you told me the Lord helps them that helps themselves! You and I sure helped ourselves to plenty of wallets on the *Robert J. Ward!*"

Nathan turned his eyes heavenward. "I've give up a life of crime, Charlie. I've found my Redeemer, and I ain't ever been so happy!"

Charlie was incredulous. "You were the best on the river, Nathan! What happened?"

"Why, I found salvation! And Charlie — you can do the same. Abandon wicked ways, renounce the fleshpots of Babylon, seek the grace of the Lord." Fervently he seized Charlie's hand. "This is the Lord's doing, Charlie — bringing you, a rascal if there ever was one, to this humble abode."

Charlie withdrew his hand. "That's a fine way to talk about an old friend! Nathan, I've reformed too. I've got me a job as a roustabout on the docks, and I earn an honest living."

It was Nathan's turn to be suspicious. "You telling the truth?"

Charlie raised his hand. "I'm straight as a die!"

104

"You was always a tricky one, Charlie! I'm not sure you always split fifty-fifty with me like we arranged. I mind one time in Memphis when you —"

"I tell you I've left all that behind me! I'm leading an honest life now. Lorna — you remember me talking about Lorna Bascomb? Well, she wanted me to make something respectable out of myself. To please her, I took up the dentist trade. It didn't work out too well and so she left me when I neglected tooth pulling for the pasteboards — said she'd never marry a gambler. But I've reformed, Nathan! Right now I'm kind of edging out west where Lorna went to her uncle's place. I — I hope maybe we can pick up again when she sees how I've changed."

Nathan shook his head. Pinching lips between thumb and forefinger, he looked warily at Charlie. "I dunno! You was a born gambler. Somewheres in the Bible it says the leopard can't change his spots."

"But I'm not any damned leopard! You'll see, Nathan." He changed the subject, seeing a crayon portrait of a child in a gilt frame on the table beside the Bible. "That Mary Anne?"

Nathan nodded, pulled the shawl about his legs and stirred the fire in the stove. It was beginning to snow. "My little gal!"

"Been ten years or more since I saw her. Grown, has she?"

"Fine-looking girl now. Got her sainted ma's coloring." Nathan looked at the clock on the wall. "Ought to be home from the parade pretty soon."

"Parade? What parade?"

"That's the one fly in my ointment, Charlie. The girl is unreasonable. She's one of them females that wants the vote. Imagine that! Women wanting the vote!"

Charlie remembered Forest Park.

"It ain't Christian, Charlie. Here she's gone and joined a band of crazy females that calls themselves Women United for the Right to Vote!" He shook his head, bowed his head on his cane. "Still and all, I'm purely grateful for Mary Anne, even if she's off on a wild goose chase with them crazy females." He took a deep breath. "Well, Charlie, you'll stay and have supper with us?"

"I'd be pleased," Charlie agreed.

Bustling in at dusk, cheeks red from the cold, ginger hair aflame in the glow of the lamp as she took off her hat, Mary Anne lit the small parlor with radiance.

"Mr. Callaway? Yes, Papa has spoken of you!"

I wonder what Nathan said, Charlie speculated.

"We are always pleased, Papa and I, to have a visitor. You see, I am so busy with my work for the Women United that I have little chance for socializing, and Papa is at home all day, which is very boring."

"I saw you today, ma'am," Charlie remarked. "And listened to you, too. That was a good speech you gave in Forest Park."

She was surprised. Putting on her apron to cook supper, she said, "Oh! You were there?"

"Yes, ma'am."

"Do you believe in women's suffrage, Mr. Callaway?"

Trapped, he stammered. "Well, I — I —"

"Few men do, I know!" She laughed. "Well, our time will come, you will see!" A moment later they heard her clattering pots and pans in the kitchen, stoking up the fire, humming the tune of the suffragist song.

"An attractive young lady," Charlie observed.

Nathan turned a wintry eye on him. "Charlie, you always cut quite a figure with the womenfolks. I wouldn't trust you any farther than I could see you! Look — there's that shine in your eye, damn it! Now just you don't get any ideas!"

"How can you say such a thing? I've reformed, I tell you! Womanhood is sacred to me now. Mary Anne is as safe with me as if she was my sister."

"Well —" Nathan glowered, then tottered to his feet as Mary Anne called them for supper. "You can wash up your hands in the basin on the back stoop," he said.

Supper was pork chops with cream gravy, fried potatoes, and a dried-apple pie. "You're a fine cook, ma'am," Charlie complimented Mary Anne. "Best meal I've had since —" Since what? Since the Stoltzfus farm, where he had compromised Emma Stoltzfus. "Since a long time," he said lamely.

While Mary Anne did the dishes Nathan and Charlie sat in the parlor, smoking and reminiscing.

"In a way, I kind of miss the old days," Nathan said. "Still, my soul is filled with other things nowadays — the love of the Lord, for instance. But I sure miss the money." He waved his hand around the parlor. "Mary Anne and I are about broke. Oh, she clerks in a shipping firm, but it don't pay much, and I don't bring in anything. There's a mortgage payment due on this place, and we don't have the money to pay it."

"Maybe I can help," Charlie offered.

"How?"

"I don't know — yet."

"Something crooked, I bet," Nathan grumbled. "Well, here's my girl!"

Mary Anne came in then to join them, a lovely dew on her forehead from the heat of the kitchen. Touching it with a lacy handkerchief, she kissed Nathan and then sat down on the sofa across from Charlie. "You were — partners in the old days with Papa, Mr. Callaway?"

"Ah — yes, ma'am. But I've seen the error of sinful ways, like your pa. I'm an honest — well, I guess you could call me a laborer, a workingman, kind of a mechanic, now."

"I'm glad. And I am so glad Papa has taken up a new way of life!"

Nathan mumbled something under his breath. It sounded to Charlie like "It don't pay the bills, though."

"We are poor people," Mary Anne went on, "but honest, now, and hard-working. I am sure we will come out all right in the end."

"And how is the suffrage movement coming along, ma'am?"

Mary Anne sighed, brushed a vagrant red-gold strand of hair from her cheek. "Money is a problem there, too, Mr. Callaway."

"Call me Charlie, ma'am. I am an old friend of the family."

108

"Charlie, then, if you please. Women United always needs money. There are placards to be made, paints and paper and pencils to be bought, money for travel on the cars to the state legislature in Jefferson City to persuade our elected representatives — oh, it takes so much! But in spite of all our efforts, I fear that the suffragist movement will fail unless we come upon some funds very soon."

Charlie rubbed his chin thoughtfully. "I see."

Nathan yawned, blinked rheumy eyes. "Getting past my bedtime. Charlie, you got lodgings?"

"No," he admitted. "I — I'm a little down on my luck right now. An honest life is sometimes a penurious existence."

Nathan chuckled. "You always did have a flossy way with words, you scoundrel!" He turned to Mary Anne. "Daughter, do you mind giving Charlie a blanket and having him sleep in the shed out back?"

"Why, no, Papa! He is welcome!"

"Nothing in there but some old junk," Nathan went on. "But there's hay in the mow, and the cat keeps down rats. Good night, all!" At the doorway he paused. "Remember what I said," he told Charlie, and closed the door after him.

Mary Anne asked, "Whatever did Papa mean by that?"

Charlie took out his sweet potato. "Oh, it's just an old joke Nathan and I had when we were on the river." He blew a soft romantic note. "How does that suffragist tune go, Miss Mary Anne? Maybe I can get the hang of it."

She smiled. "You must call me just Mary Anne, then — Charlie."

With a lantern Mary Anne Goodbody led him to the shed in back of the house; Charlie carried blankets and a pillow. Inside, the stable smelled of hay and leather, ancient horse-stalings. "It's not a hotel," she smiled, "but I'm sure you'll be very comfortable, Charlie. The roosters start to crow at around six in the morning and will probably wake you. Whenever you're ready come in and wash up and I'll cook sausage and eggs for you and Papa."

In the rays of the lantern the ginger hair was an aureole of gold about the sensitive features. Class, Charlie thought. Mary Anne has class. Aloud, he said, "Thank you, Mary Anne. I'm sure I'll be comfortable." Ruefully he laughed. "I've slept in a lot of worse places since I've been so down on my luck!"

Rolled in the blanket, burrowing deep into the hay, he slept well, waking to a dreary dawn rent by the cacophony of the neighbor's chickens. Rubbing his eyes, he sat up. Where was he? Hay? A barn? Where in the world —

At last he remembered. Having been so many places of late, he was confused. But this must be Nathan Goodbody's place; Mary Anne and a good breakfast were waiting. Hastily he dressed and climbed down the ladder from the haymow.

He paused before a large trunk over which hung a wall cabinet with a cracked mirror. One boot on the chest, he tried to rake his hair into some sort of order.

Finished, he looked thoughtfully at the trunk, lifted it by one shabby handle. Of course; this was Nathan's old trunk he took along on the boats! Lifting the lid, he drew in his breath. Here was the residue of the old man's gambling career; rolls of bogus lottery tickets, a box of fan-tan counters, several shiny metal cups containing eccentric dice — amused, Charlie rolled a pair. There were deck after deck of playing cards, good old Steamboat cards from A. Daugherty of New York City, a small roulette wheel equipped with hidden magnets to control the spin, a handsome waistcoat wadded into a ball. When he shook it out in a cloud of dust it revealed at least a half-dozen hidden pockets to conceal a "cold deck."

"It's a shame," Charlie murmured, "that you had to go holy on me, Nathan, and let all this go to waste!"

Carefully he picked up a deluxe card trimmer, a beautiful instrument of brass and steel used to shave the edges of certain cards to make them easy to find in a cut. "Still sharp," he muttered, testing his thumb on the blade.

A small fitted case contained vial after vial of colored dyes, useful to give a slightly different sheen to the floral designs of the backs of certain cards, a sheen that could be seen only if the gambler wore blue-tinted spectacles. "Nathan," Charlie breathed, "you were the best. You were the king!" He started as he heard his name called. "Eh?"

From the back stoop Mary Anne summoned him. In frilly apron, she gestured with a spatula. "I thought you were awake! Come in and have breakfast with Papa!"

111

High-stepping through new snow so his shabby boots would not leak, he sloshed water on his face and hands after breaking the scum of ice on the basin, and toweled himself dry. Inside, the kitchen smelled of eggs and sausages. He sat down and reached for a sausage but Mary Anne put a gentle hand on his. "Papa says grace first!"

Nathan said grace, adding a request to the Deity that Charlie Callaway be given strength to resist evil ways. Charlie shifted uncomfortably but said a loud amen. Afterward, they drank coffee and talked.

"I'll be sad to leave this old house," Mary Anne mused. "Papa and I have lived here for four years, and it's the first real home I ever had. Papa — well, he traveled so much, you know, and I was kept in boarding school."

Nathan sighed heavily. "Dear child, I neglected you, that's God's truth! Bent on sin, I left you to an institution. Miss Jenkins's was a good school, I'll give you that, and from dishonest earnings I was able to pay the tariff. But you turned out fine, my lass, in spite of a father's dereliction of duty." He turned to Charlie. "Didn't she?"

Charlie was ruminating.

"Didn't she?" Nathan repeated.

"Oh! Yes. Yes, indeed!"

"Only now I haven't got any money to buy beans and bacon and pay the mortgage." Nathan shook his head, dabbed at his eyes with the corner of the tablecloth.

"Now don't you worry, Papa!" Mary Anne patted her father's hand. "We — both the Goodbody family and the movement — are practically penniless, but there is one more chance, at least for the movement."

"What's that?" Charlie asked.

"We suffragists intend to give a musicale here next week. Hazel Wainwright plays the violin and Mrs. Hardesty the flute. Pauline Bixby sings beautifully. There will be cake and coffee, and we will ask for contributions. We hope it will be successful so we can keep the struggle going. What do you think, Mr. Callaway? I — I mean — Charlie?"

Charlie had dismal memories of a musical evening at Lorna Bascomb's cousin Sidney's house in Baltimore. Ladies played flutes and sang mournful songs about languishing maidens while the gentlemen shifted in chairs, crossed and uncrossed their legs, yawned, scratched, and occasionally dozed. Still, he spoke gallantly. "Why, that's a good idea! I know several eloquent passages from *The Merchant of Venice* and *Hamlet*. Perhaps you might care to have me recite them!"

"Oh, would you!" Mary Anne clasped her hands in delight. "That would be awfully nice!"

Nathan eyed him warily but Charlie went on. "Look — we can make signs and put them in shop windows. We can paint a banner and string it along the front porch. We'll decorate the house with bunting. Christmas is coming and people will be in a generous mood!"

"My goodness!" Mary Anne's eyes sparkled as she clasped her hands to her bosom. "Yes, indeed! Why, I'll go tell Pauline and Hazel and Mrs. Hardesty and

113

Thelma and all the rest right away, so we can start practicing."

In Baltimore the gentlemen had shifted in their chairs, crossed and uncrossed legs, yawned, scratched, and occasionally dozed! St. Louis men, Charlie speculated, were no different from Baltimore men. They would be bored to tears and welcome diversion while a fat lady played a flute. Helping Mary Anne wash the breakfast dishes, he looked out into the dark storm clouds over the city.

"It's in a good cause," he argued heavenward. "You can't fault me on that, can you? Do you want this attractive female and her devout pa to be turned out on the street? And what have you got against women voting, anyway?"

Mary Anne, wringing out the dishcloth, was staring at him. "Whatever are you mumbling?"

Embarrassed, Charlie essayed a small laugh. "Ah — just going over a speech from *Hamlet*. Maybe you will remember it." Striking a pose, he spoke:

> *Whether 'tis nobler in the mind to suffer*
> *The slings and arrows of outrageous fortune,*
> *Or to take arms against a sea of troubles,*
> *And by opposing, end them?*

"We'll take arms!" he cried, "and end your troubles! Just trust me, Mary Anne! Trust me!"

There was a warning peal of thunder, but Charlie in his enthusiasm looked on it as mere coincidence.

Lorna's Uncle Matthew died suddenly of an apoplexy. The mission he had labored to establish was without funds; actually, there was only enough money to give the old man a decent burial. Aunt Carrie wanted the funeral to take place at the Church of the Redeemer in the Western Addition where the Hewitts lived. But a delegation of Chinese walked all the way out to the Hewitt residence, begging Aunt Carrie to hold the last rites in Little China, where Matthew Hewitt had long been loved and respected.

"I think," Lorna said, "that Uncle Matthew would have wanted it that way, Aunt Carrie."

Aunt Carrie, gaunt and sad in rusty black, twisted a handkerchief in her hands. "It — it don't seem — well, *Christian*, Lorna!"

"Auntie, it is the most Christian thing in the world! Remember — Jesus came to the poor, the sick, the oppressed, the least of these'!"

Aunt Carrie took a deep breath. "Well, I suppose you are right."

Uncle Matthew's simple coffin was carried through the streets of Little China on the backs of poverty-stricken parishioners. Lorna and her aunt walked behind the coffin, ears assaulted by the shrill cries of the pall-bearers chanting Cantonese praise of the late Reverend Matthew Hewitt. Others bore homemade banners proclaiming the virtues of the deceased, and strings of firecrackers went off like rounds from the newly invented Gatling gun that had lately been described in the *Chronicle*. The child prostitute Loi San held Lorna's

115

hand as they marched toward the corner of Waverly Place and Washington Street. There the pallbearers put down the coffin and covered it with paper flowers. Paper money, cunningly folded paper houses, paper replicas of food and drink — all were piled in the middle of the street and burned. The symbolic gifts were thus sent to heaven for the Reverend Hewitt's use in the celestial kingdom.

The wealthy merchants of Chinatown, the *boo how doy*, the well-dressed pimps watched the ceremony with amusement. Matthew Hewitt had been an interloper in their midst, a man they feared might cause trouble among the poor and so threaten their own standing. Lorna, comforting the weeping Dah Pah Tsin, saw movement at a window. She glanced up to see Little Pete himself beaming down from the garish red and yellow building with the upswept dragon eaves that was his office — the center of power in Chinatown. Little Pete was amused. He smoked a long pipe and sneered. Some of his retainers crowded around, pointing scornful fingers and jeering at the procession.

Lorna's eyes hardened, her jaw set. In the cacophony of noise — singsong chants, exploding firecrackers, the cries of mourners — she made up her mind. After Reverend Hewitt was properly buried in the Prince of Peace Cemetery in the Western Addition, she m ade tea and passed around Aunt Carrie's oatmeal-raisin cookies to friends who had come to pay their respects. When they had left she turned to Aunt Carrie.

"Auntie, I have something to tell you."

Aunt Carrie stopped rocking. "Yes, dear."

"All of Uncle Matthew's work is not going for naught if I can help it!"

"Child, what do you mean?"

"With all respect, Auntie, I am not a child, I tell you! And while I do not have a man's strength or knowledge, I intend to keep the mission open!"

"What?"

"Yes, I mean it!"

"But — but where will you get the money, dear? It will be a problem even to keep this old house and provide food for the two of us!"

"We will manage," Lorna said. "The Lord brought manna to the Israelites in the desert when they were starving. It is in Exodus somewhere — 'The children of Israel did eat manna for forty years.' Remember?"

The old lady shook her head, resumed her rocking. "Lorna, I am too distraught and confused to think. Later on, perhaps, we can talk about it."

CHAPTER
SEVEN

Preparations went on apace for the Suffragist Christmas Musicale at the Goodbody house. Mary Anne's ladies cleaned, painted the parlor, made a banner to string across the front porch of the house, baked cookies, worried over the kind of punch to serve their guests. A string quartet sat in the parlor, sawing away. Nathan put his fingers in his ears and finally retired to his room. The ladies still wanted to distribute handbills advertising the event, but there was not enough money in the till. Charlie came to the rescue.

"I'll get another job."

"But where? This is winter, and trade has slowed down something awful."

"Trust me," he told Mary Anne.

Trade *was* slow. In one of the coldest winters the city had experienced, the river was filled with floating chunks of ice that would damage a steamboat hull. Shipping had almost ceased and the steamboat crews were laid off. They spent their time drinking in the beer, gardens and engaging in fistfights. As a consequence, a lot of teeth were broken off and knocked out. When Charlie applied to Dr. Bleecker's Dental Emporium, he was immediately hired.

"Got more business than I can handle," the septuagenarian wheezed. "You a good dentist?"

"Good enough."

"Where did you learn the trade?"

"Honor graduate of Dr. Motherwell's College of Dentistry and Animal Husbandry in Baltimore!"

The old man blew his nose on his sleeve. "Never heard of it, but I ain't in condition to be picky." He nodded toward the other dental chair. "Go to work!"

The pay was meager — three dollars a day — but it would buy paint for the dining room, pressed also into service for the crowd expected, pay a printer's bill, purchase a large punch bowl. Mary Anne, exultant, kissed him on the cheek. "Oh, thank you, Charlie!"

"Yes, ma'am," he said, watching her dance gaily about the room waving the colorful handbills. The place on his cheek where she had kissed him was warm; it seemed somehow to retain the imprint of her lips. Softly he touched the place, caught up in reverie. It always seemed to be a long time since he had been with a woman.

"Eh?" He jumped.

Nathan looked somberly over the rims of his spectacles. "Something on your mind?"

"No," Charlie said hastily. "Just — just woolgathering, I guess."

"There ain't no sheep in this house, remember that!"

"It was just a figure of speech, Nathan."

"Well, stop figuring and pick up a paint brush!"

In a final burst of activity the ladies decorated a Christmas tree in one corner of the parlor and strung spiraled red ribbons from the ceiling. Charlie had made his preparations also.

"Why do you spend every evening in that old shed?" Mary Anne asked. "It's cold out there!"

"Meditating. It's a practice common among the holy men of India. After a hard day pulling teeth, I find it rests me."

She peered at him. "Charlie, is there something wrong with your eyes? Look at me!"

Guiltily he said, "Ah — perhaps it's the ether I have to use in difficult extractions. It seems to inflame the eyeballs."

"Well, you must do something about it! Papa has an eyewash that is very good."

The ladies were in a flush of expectation. When seven o'clock sounded they were in best finery, hovering near the door. Nathan wore a rusty black frock coat; his bearded chin was propped high on a paper collar. "I can't hardly breathe!" he confided to Charlie. The old man had loaned Charlie a clean shirt and a moth-eaten velvet jacket. The jacket smelled musty, but Charlie did not intend to spend too much time in the parlor.

"Here comes someone!" Pauline giggled, peering through the window.

"It's Mr. and Mrs. Goebel!" Mary Anne decided.

Mary Anne and Pauline Bixby constituted the receiving line, shaking hands with the arrivals.

"Mrs. Baker — and you've brought Henry! Why, here are the Bachmanns! Papa, shake hands with Mr. Bachmann. He's Bachmann's Livery Stable. And Mrs. Bachmann!"

120

More and more guests came. "Pauline, show Mr. and Mrs. Anderson to the punch and cookies. Help yourself, folks! In a few minutes we will have some musical selections. Henrietta, how nice of you to come!"

The ladies were pleasant but the gentlemen seemed unwilling captives. I was right, Charlie thought, blowing spit from his ocarina in preparation for his musical number, a rousing rendition of "Hail, Columbia!"

The attendance was more than expected, and Mary Anne was thrilled. But when she made her opening remarks, the response was restrained.

"We know you are all fair-minded ladies and gentlemen, and hope you will agree that females are the equal of men in everything but physical strength. We cook, sew, and do laundry. We also think, have opinions, and are citizens of this republic, just as men are. So our society will continue to fight the good fight for the sake of the women of America! But it is an expensive proposition, and we need money. You will find a large basket on a stand by the door. As you leave after the program, I hope you will open your hearts and your wallets, gentlemen, and by so doing espouse the great cause that is dear to the hearts of your helpmates!"

There was a spattering of applause. Several of the gentlemen squirmed in their chairs. Some appeared to enjoy Charlie's lively solo, but the squirming became contagious when Mrs. Hardesty sang "Mother Is in Heaven — What a Bright Angel She Will Be!" While the string quartet was assaulting a work of Johann Sebastian Bach, Charlie retired to the hallway. Eyeing

121

the bored gentlemen, he crooked a finger at a stocky man with a wealth of black beard and gold pince-nez who looked prosperous.

"Pssst!"

The gentleman stared, then muttered an excuse to his wife. Mopping his forehead with a handkerchief, he whispered, "What's up?"

"Boring, isn't it?" Charlie asked.

"Mabel made me come."

"Like a little action?"

The heavy brows drew together. "What do you mean?"

"Go out the back way to the shed on the alley. There's a lamp burning there. I'll pass the word to a few others. Wait for me!"

Surreptitiously Charlie attracted the attention of others, waiting between each so as not to give the game away.

"Right out the back door, gentlemen. Join the rest. I'll be along in a minute."

Bach having been disposed of, the ladies mounted a campaign against Beethoven. Quietly Charlie withdrew, joining the little group around the roulette wheel in the shed. Taking off the moth-eaten coat, he rolled up his sleeves. "Everyone likes a little action, gentlemen, and remember, it's for a good cause. Miss Mary Anne Goodbody needs help, but there isn't any reason why you gentlemen can't have a little fun for your money, is there?" He spun the wheel. "There's a bottle of prime Kentucky whiskey on the sawhorse there and more to

122

follow. Wet your whistles, men. That suffragist punch was deadly!"

Passing the bottle, they crowded around the sawhorse. "I was that dry!" the black-bearded gentleman complained, shaking hands with Charlie. "I'm Joshua Loomis."

"Nothing like lady fiddlers to parch you, Mr. Loomis," Charlie agreed. "Now make your bets, fellows! Red or black — high or low! It's your choice, men! Zero or double zero? The little ball bounces, and where she stops no one knows!"

In fact, no one knew but Charlie and the magnets in the wheel. "A dollar on red! Five dollars on black! Number seventeen, sir? Your lucky number! Here she goes!" He spun the wheel. "The bank gives good odds, folks! Thirty-five to one if your number comes up! Think of it!"

No winning number came up, although one player won on red at even-money odds. Charlie raked in the bills. "Just the first twirl, gentlemen! This is the wheel of fortune, right enough! There's wealth in this wheel — winning numbers are all over it like a plague of ants! Try again — pick a number, a color, a combination if you wish!"

Huddled around the wheel, their faces were intent in the hooded glow of the lamp. The bottle passed around again and was emptied; Charlie cracked a fresh one. The liquor had cost him dear but it was necessary.

"Here she goes, gents! Round and round, spinning fortunes for the lucky ones! Hey, hey! Clickety-click she goes, and the little ball rolls and rolls!"

This time he collected eleven dollars and had to pay out six. Joshua Loomis complained but took out another five-dollar bill. "I usual have luck at the cards, but this danged wheel ain't very good to me!"

In a half hour the wheel was forty-eight dollars ahead. Some of the players were unhappy. Joshua Loomis, glowering, asked, "You sure this is an honest wheel?"

"Sure it is!" someone said thickly, wiping his mouth and passing the bottle. "Don't be a poor sport, Josh! Why, Loomis Iron Works charges enough for boiler repairs! You ain't hurting for cash!"

The gaming went on, well-lubricated with Kentucky bourbon. Charlie's voice grew hoarse from his patter. Nathan's borrowed shirt was damp with sweat even though it was snowing outside and frost spangled the alley window. "Don't be downhearted, gents! Remember — one lucky number and you get it all back, and more! Make your bets, men! Pick a number, a color, whatever you fancy!"

By now he had sixty-nine dollars in his pocket but the liquor was running short. One of the gamblers had fallen asleep in a pile of hay. Another dozed against a post, hands folded in his lap. Loomis — Mr. Joshua Loomis? Charlie looked around. Loomis had vanished. Uneasily Charlie made an announcement. "Gents, this is the final spin! All good things must come to an end!" Was Loomis going to cause trouble?

"All good things!" someone snorted. "Callaway, where did you get that wheel? I think it's crooked! Already I lost eighteen dollars, and —"

Disaster arrived simultaneously from both ends of the stable. Carrying a lamp, holding up her skirt with one hand so as to clear the snow in the back yard, Mary Anne Goodbody opened one door, asking, "Where are all the menfolks? My goodness — there's nothing but ladies in the parlor!" At the same time the alley door creaked open. Mr. Joshua Loomis pointed out Charlie Callaway to a burly constable.

"There he is, officer! Arrest him! He's running a crooked game in this stable!"

Charlie did not stand on ceremony. Hesitating only a moment to choose between the two doors, he bolted for the alley, knocking down Loomis and bowling over the constable. They were both bigger than he was but he had the advantage of great velocity. In the alley he sprawled over a trash barrel, scrambled to his feet, plastered with mud and snow, and hurdled a fence. Dogs barked, windows flew up, the constable and victims of the magnetized wheel hallooed after him. A wicked cur in the alley bit him on the ankle. Muttering an imprecation, he kicked out but lost part of a pants leg. Running into a thorny bush, he struggled and then relaxed, aware that the hanging posse had gone by and was baying its prey on the wrong trail. Breathing a sigh of relief, he was gingerly freeing himself from the thorny embrace of the bush when a window above creaked open. A night-capped head appeared, directly below which was the muzzle of a shotgun.

"Who's down there?"

Charlie froze.

"I see you — in my rose bushes!"

"Wait a minute!" Charlie pleaded, trying to think of a reason why he would be in a man's rose bushes during the night. "I'm a city inspector! Have you noticed that you've built a foot too close to the property line? I —"

The shotgun muzzle bloomed into a flower of smoke and flame. Through the borrowed shirt Charlie felt something sting. Blundering through the yard, he ran into the next street, hearing a lot of yelling from the pack that had lost his trail. Now they were backtracking on him. Legs rubbery, lungs laboring, he tottered across the street and into another alley. Finding a swaybacked outhouse behind a small cottage, he opened the door and sat down, pulling the door to after him.

The sounds of pursuit dwindled. For the moment at least, he was safe and he had the money. Sixty-nine dollars bulked large in his pants pocket. But in the odorous darkness of the privy he saw again the shock and surprise in Mary Anne Goodbody's eyes, and was desolate.

The next morning, with what remained of his own money, he bought a new pair of pants, another shirt, and a warm coat. After washing off the night's mud in a riverfront bathhouse and paying for a shave, he looked almost presentable, although his hide still stung from random birdshot. In the wan gray light of a winter morning he composed a note to Mary Anne Goodbody.

Dear Mary Anne:

I am sorry Things turned out as they Did. I meant well, but my Old Ways betrayed me. Anyway, I wanted you to know that I meant Well

126

and it was Fate that did me in. I am Enclosing sixty-nine Dollars which I Hope will help you in your Fight for the Vote.

Charlie Callaway

For a moment he chewed on the pencil, then added:

Please give my Best Regards to your papa. I am Glad he has given up his former Evil Ways. This has been a Lesson to me too. I intend to do Good Works for the rest of my Life as penance for my many Misdeeds.

Feeling better, he put the note in an envelope with the sixty-nine dollars and walked to Nathan Goodbody's house. It was a bitterly cold morning and frigid air burned his cheeks. Few were on the streets; only a dray wagon of coal passed, driver bundled like a cocoon and the horses breathing plumes of steam. It was early, very early; he guessed that Nathan and Mary Anne were still in bed. Glancing around, he tiptoed up the steps to slip the envelope under the door. He was bent over in the act when the door came open.

"Charlie!"

He stiffened and rose slowly, holding the envelope.

"How — how dare you come back here after what you've done! I have a mind to call the police!" Mary Anne's long red hair was done up in curlpapers and she wore a cotton wrapper. Still she was beautiful, even in her wrath. "How can you — can you —"

"Shhh! Do you want to wake everyone?" He handed her the envelope. "Just take this and I'll go away, Mary Anne!"

"What is it?"

"Money! A lot of money!"

She drew herself up. "Tainted money! Take it back! I wouldn't touch anything dishonestly gained!"

He refused the envelope. "Don't be foolish, Mary Anne! The Lord moves in mysterious ways. That's in the Bible somewhere. Just look at it this way — maybe I was only the Lord's instrument!"

She started to weep. "Oh, Charlie! Why do you have to be such a rascal? You're a smart man, an intelligent man, a — a very charming man! You don't have to cheat and swindle. You could make something of yourself in honest ways."

"It's a weakness," Charlie admitted. Hearing noises from inside, he realized that Nathan was getting up. He did not want to talk to Nathan.

"I — I was beginning to like-you, Charlie! I — I felt good around you! But then —"

Her lip trembled, the full and inviting lip. Charlie seized her in his arms, pressed her bosom against his own, kissed her hard on the lips. Then, aghast at his own daring, he fled. As he blundered away he heard Nathan Goodbody's querulous voice.

"Where did he go, Mary Anne? I swear, I'll wear that rascal out with a pick handle!"

Later, sitting before a schooner of beer in a smoky waterfront saloon, he was despondent. He had meant well, as always. All he ever wanted was to help Mary

128

Anne and her campaign for the vote, though he had some doubts that women were entitled to it. Still, he had brought disaster on himself. Maybe Mary Anne was right. Perhaps he could succeed without chicanery. It was a bizarre thought, but he might give it a try. "Maybe I just possibly saw a streak of good — just a pinch, mind you — in your miserable soul"; that was what the Old Gentleman said. Mary Anne Goodbody must have seen some good in him, too. Now, he realized, was a turning point in his life. He must react to it, or sink forever into a sea of deceit and sin. Squaring his shoulders, he paid one of his last coins for the beer and walked out on the levee, being immediately confronted by an out-of-tune threesome; a man puffing a battered tuba, another with a squeaky fife, and a third banging a drum. Behind them straggled a few waterfront derelicts.

"What's all this?" Charlie asked a bleary-eyed follower who smelled powerfully of cheap whiskey.

"Mission."

"What?"

The man hiccuped, caught at Charlie's lapel to steady himself. "Reverend Purdy's Mission, up on O'Fallon Street. He gives you soup and bread, but first you got to listen to a sermon."

Charlie joined the procession. The Lamb of God Mission was an abandoned warehouse, damp and musty-smelling, and the small potbellied stove did little to dispel the chill. He sat on a wooden bench with the other lost souls, listening to Reverend Purdy, a gaunt and spectral prophet who knew all about hellfire and enlightened them with conviction.

"You got to *fear* God! Yes, that's what the Good Book says! You got to get the fear of the Lord in your very bones before you can abandon sinful ways and come to salvation! Whoo-ee, brothers! The great day is coming when the Lord Jehovah is going to separate the sheep from the goats! You better take warning and cleanse your sinful souls! Praise God! Oh, yes — praise God!"

Lorna Bascomb had tried to lead Charlie to salvation but somewhere along the way he had lost the path. He tried earnestly to listen to the Reverend Purdy, but lack of sleep the previous night gradually weakened him; he dozed, waking only when there was a great shuffling of feet and an exodus to the kitchen where Mrs. Purdy presided over a cauldron of soup — a lot of vegetables with a few chunks of fatty meat in a thin broth. Charlie dipped stale bread in the soup, feeling the rumbling in his stomach finally subside. Afterward, in gratitude, he stayed to help Reverend and Mrs. Purdy wash the dishes and clean up.

"You're a bright, presentable young man," Purdy observed. "What brings you to this low estate, young man?"

"Fate," Charlie said. "An unkind fate."

"I've heard that line before. Drink, was it? Women? Gambling?"

Charlie winced. "Maybe a little of all of them."

His help won him a cot and a ragged blanket on the second floor that night, along with a dozen or so smelly vagrants as bedfellows. Cautiously he put his shoes under the pillow and slept in his clothes. If this was the way to start to lead an exemplary life, it was not very satisfactory. In an atmosphere of raucous snores, dirty feet, and beery exhalations, he finally slept — and had a nightmare.

Finally he had found the perfect holdout. It could not fail. In his mind's eye he saw clearly the mechanical details — the harness of pulleys, cords, and telescoping metal tubes. The jointed frame reached from his forearm to his shoulder, thence down to his knees. Worn inside the clothing, the contraption could be adjusted to any man's girth or height. To activate the holdout all a gambler had to do was spread his knees and a claw holding an extra ace would move unseen out of the sleeve into his hand. It was marvelous — the greatest thing since the telegraph, the locomotive, the cotton gin!

Fondly he articulated the machine, exulting in the sinuous way the metal skeleton moved silently, effectively, extending the ace of spades into his hand. Lorna was pulling at his sleeve, weeping.

"No, Charlie! No! Please!"

Roughly he pushed her aside. "This is a hard world, Lorna! A man has got to make a stake before he can get married. This is for you, Lorna — believe me!"

When Lorna picked up a hammer and tried to destroy his machine — the perfect holdout — he snatched her wrist and twisted till she dropped the hammer.

"You don't understand! You just don't understand! It's all right! I'm only doing it so we can get married!"

But Lorna, weeping, ran away. Desolate, he turned back to the holdout. Now it was acting very strangely. It seemed to have developed a mind of it own. Without his aid it was moving through a kind of bizarre dance — joints rotating, springs stretching and shortening, the metal claw held menacingly aloft. Shrinking back, he ducked as the claw tried for his head.

"Here!" he said, sternly. "What's going on here!"

On metal legs the holdout clambered down from the table and tottered toward him, claw outstretched. Terrified, he ran, the machine lumbering after him. Sleek, oiled, and silent; its deadly quietness was horrifying.

"No!" he begged. "Stay away from me! Oh, don't! Please don't."

Fast as he ran, the holdout was faster. It cornered him, blocking his exit. The deadly claw opened and shut before his eyes, like the tooth-studded maw of a crocodile. "No!" he yelled, cowering in a corner. "Don't kill me — please! I repent! Yes, I repent!"

Someone was shaking his shoulder. Bathed in sweat, trembling, he woke to find a skinny man in a flowered vest and little else holding a candle over him.

"What in hell you yelling about, feller? You'd wake the dead!"

Charlie took a deep shuddering breath. "I — I repent," he muttered, still half caught up in the dream.

"Well, repent somewheres else!" a voice called. "God damn it — can't a man get no sleep anymore?"

Reverend Purdy's mission served only one meal a day, at noon, but because of his helpfulness Charlie was invited to breakfast with the Purdys. It was scanty — cornmeal mush and sorghum molasses, along with weak coffee.

132

"We ain't got much but the Lord's blessing," Reverend Purdy observed after saying grace. "Times are hard, and sometimes the Devil tempts the missus and me to give up." Sipping coffee, he looked at Charlie Callaway. "I hear you had a bad dream last night."

"It was a vision. Kind of a warning, like. Reverend, it changed my life. From now on I'm redeemed. I intend to lead a Christian life and join the happy throng of the saved."

"Hallelujah!"

"Yes, I've seen the burning pit of hell!"

"Praise God!"

"I've come up into the sunlight of salvation!"

The Purdys were ecstatic.

"Yes, sir, and yes, ma'am, I've had a sign!"

"Thank the Lord!"

They pulled him to his knees and the Purdys prayed, thanking the Lord for the saving of a poor sinner.

"For," Reverend Purdy said, "the Lord rejoices more over one lost sheep than a whole barnful of the found!"

"Well, now I'm found!" Grateful to the Purdys, he asked, "You're short of funds, eh?"

Purdy sighed. "If something don't come in soon, Maude and I will have to close the mission. Rent's due next week, and we ain't got but three dollars in the till."

Charlie remembered Mary Anne Goodbody's words: "Charlie, you're a smart man, an intelligent man! You don't have to cheat and swindle! You could make something of yourself in honest ways!" That was what Lorna had always said, too. Encouraged by salvation, he began to believe in himself. He had given up cheating and swindling, but he was a sharp poker player even at a straight game, and the laid-off steamboat men idled away their time playing five-card stud in the waterfront dives.

"Reverend, that vision of mine was powerful! The Lord spoke to me. He said you should trust me to invest that three dollars."

Mrs. Purdy's brow wrinkled. "Invest?"

"With the Lord's help, I promise to bring back ten dollars for every one dollar you lay in my hand!"

Reverend Purdy shook his head. "I don't know —"

"I swear it'll work! The good Lord himself told me so! Don't you believe in visions?"

Mrs. Purdy sighed. "Purdy, three dollars ain't going to get us anywhere anyways. If this nice young man has had a vision —"

Reverend Purdy took a cigar box from a shelf and handed Charlie three dollars, leaving a small amount of change in the box. "Son, there's something about you that tells me you're honest! No man could get saved as loud and convincing as you without being a good man, an honest man, at heart. Go forth and challenge the forces of evil! We'll be praying for you — and for the dividends from our investment!"

Hastening forth, Charlie was not long in confronting the forces of evil. In a five-card stud game at Hennessy's Saloon on the waterfront, he won sixteen dollars in a little over an hour, drawing suspicious stares from the burly steamboat men.

"Lucky ain't you, stranger?" a bearded tough with a knife scar across his cheek sneered.

"Skill," Charlie said modestly. Well ahead now, he bought drinks for the other players, along with a ham sandwich for himself. Breakfast had not been filling. "Drink up, gents! Maybe your luck will change!"

In the smoky half light through the dirty windows he continued to win. Knife Scar demanded a new deck and began to retrieve some of the money Charlie had won. In fact, whenever Knife Scar dealt he seemed to win. Charlie, fortified with integrity himself, began to suspect Knife Scar of cheating. Folding his cards into a tight pack, he realized at once that the edges of certain cards had been subtly rounded; the "corner rounder" was a small machine with an ivory-handled blade that he had often used himself in former days. What to do?

Knife Scar won again on his deal. Charlie made up his mind. Don't it say in the Bible "An eye for an eye and a tooth for a tooth"?

"What you mumbling about?" Knife Scar demanded.

"Just a habit!" Charlie explained. "Harmless, really."

On the next deal he sequestered the ace of hearts, slipping it expertly into his sleeve when he picked up his cards. Dropping early so his four-card hand would not be noticed, he flipped his other cards into the pile in the center of the table while Knife Scar raked in his pile.

Cheater! Charlie thought piously. Scoundrel! I'll fix your wagon!

He won the next hand with a pair of aces and a jack kicker. Knife Scar was incredulous when he lost with two kings. Sullen, he stared at Charlie. "Where you come from, brother?"

"Oh, lots of places. Washington, D.C., mostly."

"There are a lot of crooks there, besides the politicians."

"Oh my, yes!" Charlie agreed. "How many cards to you, sir?"

It isn't cheating, he argued to himself. Honest! It's just — well, fighting fire with fire!

Disaster came quickly. Charlie was forty-one dollars ahead when Knife Scar suddenly announced, "There's an ace missing from this deck! The ace of spades!"

There was indeed; Charlie had it in his sleeve.

"How do you know?" someone demanded.

Leering, Knife Scar spread out the cards. "There? Anyone see the ace of spades?"

The atmosphere became ugly. One man rose, drawing a knife from the sheath at his belt. Another pulled a snub-nosed derringer. The bartender, anticipating violence, picked up a bung starter and hurried over to the table.

"What's going on here, gents? A little trouble?"

Charlie picked up his ham sandwich, took a large bite. "It appears there is a missing card."

Knife Scar leaned over the table, staring at Charlie, his massive fists planted on the green baize. "And I know where it is!"

Charlie took another bite of the sandwich. "You do?"

"I damn well do!"

As he was pushing more of the sandwich into his mouth Knife Scar grabbed him by the collar and jerked him to his feet. "Search him!" he ordered a crony. "Take off his coat and pants!"

136

Continuing to chew, Charlie stood docilely while they stripped him.

"Satisfied?" he asked with dignity.

Knife Scar swore. "I was certain —"

"How about the rest of you gentlemen?" Charlie demanded. "Fair's fair, isn't it? I let you search *me* and you didn't find any ace of spades!"

"That's right!" the bartender said. "We don't allow no crooked games in here!" He hefted the bung starter ominously. "You gents — take off your clothes!"

A crowd had gathered, delighted. They jeered and snickered while the rest of the cardplayers sullenly took off shirts, pants, shoes, drawers, to stand shivering in the river chill. The ace of spades had disappeared.

"Probably fell through a crack in the floor," Charlie remarked. Indeed, there were wide cracks in the plank floor. "Now let that teach you a lesson, men, not to accuse honest citizens of cheating!" Tipping his hat haughtily, he walked out of Hennessy's Saloon. In the street a safe distance away, he spat out the remnants of the ace of spades he had slipped into the ham sandwich. As a precaution he bought a bottle of Dr. Weaver's Stomach Bitters and Dyspepsia Remedy and still returned the joyous Purdys an even thirty dollars, saving out eleven for himself.

"Praise the Lord!" Reverend Purdy cried, seeing the bills.

Charlie's stomach felt a little gaseous but he joined the chorus.

"Oh, yes! Whoo-ee! Praise the Lord!"

CHAPTER
EIGHT

Wrapped in old newspapers, sleeping in the wreckage of a great oaken cask on the river flats, Charlie let his mind wander into a delicious idyll. Lorna and he were married, and had several children; Charlie liked children. The tots played about their feet while Lorna knitted and Charlie read the evening newspaper. On the hearth a fire blazed and a tabby cat washed its face with a paw. Lorna! Ah, Lorna! His heart overflowed with love even for the cat, and he did not ordinarily care for cats. But first he had to escape St. Louis. On account of the misadventure with Nathan Goodbody's roulette wheel, the city police were probably still looking for him. Also there was the possibility of the Army still searching for a too-lucky gambler, deserter, and three-time bounty jumper.

In the dead of winter he found a job as swamper on a freight wagon bound for Kansas City. Skilled at mechanical things, he hired on as a mechanic in the Kansas City railroad yards, repairing steam gauges, turning valve gears, machining petcocks. Lorna had always liked Charlie's long slender fingers. Other signs failing, she said they were the sign of an artistic temperament. Of course, they had long been misused

138

in dishonest pursuits. Now they were dedicated to good works. He went once to church in Kansas City and prayed as loud as anyone.

The winter wore on; spring came apace. In the shop he found time to fashion a new set of dental tools to replace those lost when he hastily abandoned the North Central Railroad coach just outside of Chambersburg, in Pennsylvania. It was so long ago — or did it just seem a long time ago since his remarkable conversion? Skillfully he fashioned picks, forceps, scalpel; made a small hand drill with gears and chuck salvaged from a junk pile in the grimy shop. Finally he soldered together a tin case and looked with pride on his handiwork, the shiny instruments in felt-lined recesses. In San Francisco he would take up dentistry again to support Lorna and the several small children. The eldest — a handsome child with his hair and Lorna's coloring — would be Charles Junior. The next, a lovely little girl, would be —

He broke off, snapping the lid shut on the instruments. Dreaming would get him nowhere! Action was required; action, and dedication. San Francisco and Lorna Bascomb were two thousand miles or more in the direction of the setting sun. In the Missouri spring, as gentle rains brought out leaves on the trees and tulips waved red and yellow and white in the park at Lake Jacomo, he bought deck passage on the *Sunflower*, a side-wheeler. St. Joe was a hundred twisting sand-barred miles up the river. Emigrant trains for California and Oregon, he heard, started frequently from St. Joe, and he would sign on. With his skills as dentist, mechanic, and entertainer — he still had his sweet potato — he would certainly be welcomed.

Now the war was winding down to a bloody finale. Sheridan had routed Pickett's division and Fitzhugh Lee's cavalry at Five Forks, and the Federals had taken Petersburg and Lynchburg. Charlie arrived in St. Joe to hear that President Lincoln had been assassinated by a deranged actor in Ford's Theater on E Street, between Thirteenth and Fourteenth. Charlie had once taken Lorna there. In a blaze of gaslight they had seen a dramatic pageant titled *The Naiad Queen*. Now St. Joe, a sprawling frontier town on the east bank of the Mississippi, mourned for Mr. Lincoln. St. Joe had known bloodshed during the war, being visited by Quantrill's guerrillas and the James gang, and in former years the local Sac and Fox tribes had fought for the site as sacred burial grounds for their dead. Now the town was draped in mourning for a martyred President, the loading of immigrant wagons momentarily abandoned for prayer services in the Methodist church.

Charlie, his possessions in a secondhand carpetbag, walked the waterfront among the immigrant wagons. A detachment of soldiers was drilling on a grassy plot, and he gave them a wide berth. There were many wagons of various shapes and sizes. Some had several span of oxen; others were drawn by mules. On the sides of the wagon box and suspended from the back was a variety of items: picks, hoes, shovels, sacks of grain, lanterns, buckets, extra wheels, perhaps an extra wagon tongue. The whole structure was borne by high wheels to give plenty of clearance over rocks and other

140

obstacles, although the front wheels were smaller to permit sharp turns, the smaller wheels swiveling under the wagon box.

In a welter of braying mules, snuffling oxen, men making last-minute repairs, women calling tearful good-byes to friends, children playing tag among the high wheels, Charlie looked for a favorable situation.

"Going to California, friend?" he asked a fat man in a flowered waistcoat who was filing a mule's hoof.

"Oregon," the man said shortly.

"Need a hand to go part way? I'm a dentist down on my luck — also a good mechanic, a hard worker, and an A1 handyman into the bargain."

The man straightened. Speaking, he displayed a mouth notable for its lack of teeth. "What the hell you think I need a dentist for? Anyways, with a wife and a mother-in-law and six kids, I got all the company I need!"

He tried again. This time the wagon was headed for Sacramento but the owner demanded that in exchange for his passage Charlie buy him an extra span of oxen at ninety dollars apiece. Charlie shook his head. "I haven't got that sort of money, friend."

"Then how you expect to get took along? The trip costs money. I spent four hundred dollars so far on this rig, and still need another pair of ox critters!"

Weary and despondent, Charlie sat on a nail keg, gloomily watching departing wagons. Dusk came, and the last passage of the ferry. More wagons rolled into town, ready to leave on the morrow. Cooking fires made bright dots along the banks of the Missouri. The soft evening air was filled with the perfume of frying bacon, the sounds of fiddle, Jew's harp, and banjo. Seeing a bearded gentleman tinkering with a clock by the light of a lantern, Charlie paused.

"Good evening, sir."

The man, a patriarch with a square-cut grizzled beard and flat-brimmed black hat, looked up.

"A clock that won't run?" Charlie asked.

The old man grunted, picked at the interior of the clock with a screwdriver. "The Devil has got into this clock!"

Charlie put down the carpetbag. "I'm very good with clocks, sir. Here — let me have a look at it."

Reluctantly the old man handed it over. Charlie peered inside. "Not very much wrong," he decided. Choosing a pick from his case of dental tools, he bent a metal tab back into place and hooked the mainspring to it. "There!" Taking the key, he wound the clock; it started to tick in regular and reassuring rhythm.

"Well, I'll be danged!" the old man marveled. "Stranger, I thank you." He extended his hand. "Abner Wilfong, from Circleville, Ohio."

"Charles Chaney Callaway, from parts east."

They sat on the wagon-tongue in the moonlight, talking, while Mrs. Wilfong, a cheery gray-haired dumpling of a woman, fried potatoes and sausages over an open fire. A small towheaded child peeked out of the wagon at Charlie, and a younger woman took tin plates and cups from a box nailed to the side of the wagon. Abner Wilfong told Charlie the story of their travail.

"Left Circleville over a year ago — me and my woman, my son Harold and Sarah — that's Harold's

142

wife — and little Betsy. Farming wasn't paying. We sold the farm. Mostly stumps and rocks, it was. We bought mules and a wagon to go out to Californy. We heard there was good land for free. But the wagon busted down and Harold took a quinsy and died in Webster Grove, Missouri. Now Sarah's a widow, Betsy ain't got no pa, and Mary and me are pretty old and rickety to be taking out for Californy. Still, we ain't got no place else to go." He sighed, held the clock to his ear to confirm the satisfying tick. "We ain't got much, Mr. Callaway, but guess we can offer you supper."

"I'd be proud," Charlie agreed.

Sarah put Betsy to bed in the wagon. She and Mrs. Wilfong sat silently as Charlie and Abner Wilfong smoked a late pipe. Anticipating an early start, most of the other travelers had bedded down. There was little sound but the gentle purling of the river through the reeds near the shore.

"So," Abner Wilfong concluded, "we're going across on the ferry in the morning. After that, it's in the Lord's hands." He knocked out the dottle of the pipe. "Well —"

"Listen," Charlie said.

"Eh?"

"I've got an idea! You need a strong young man to go along. I'm pretty handy — good mechanic, hard worker, a dentist into the bargain. I want to go to California, too. Will you take me with you?"

Abner stroked his beard. "Well, I dunno —"

"I'd pay my way! I've got sixty dollars saved up!"

143

"It's a long way, and I got to admit we ain't too strong in the provisions department. We need a better water barrel — the old one is about done for, and leaks. We need leather for patching harness, and bacon and taters, too. Guess we could use another rifle or shotgun, and some powder and ball. Cornmeal, too, and a skillet to make up for the one we lost somewheres along the way." He shook his head. "Dang it, we need a *lot* of things!"

"Don't worry," Charlie said. "At first light we'll go over to the general store and buy what you need. By the time they call your number on the ferry we'll be ready to go!"

I'm on my way, Lorna! Charlie is coming, a changed man! Wait for me, Lorna!

"Who's Lorna?" Abner asked.

Charlie was startled. "Lorna?"

"You was mumbling something about Lorna, sounded like."

"I don't know," Charlie said, embarrassed, "but if you don't mind, I'll just stretch out under the wagon tonight."

He woke in a gray May dawn to find a pair of gentle blue eyes peering into his. Betsy Wilfong shook his shoulder again to make sure he was awake.

"Grandpa says the sun will be up in another few minutes, mister!"

Painfully Charlie sat up, bumping his head on the wagon axle. "Why, I thank you, Miss Betsy!"

Pleased at the status conferred, she smiled. He wanted his children to have a gap-toothed smile like that. "There's oatmeal and fried eggs ready — coffee too!" In her pinafore she bounded away through the tall grass like a fawn, singing.

"Ah, youth!" Charlie sighed, and staggered to his feet, folded his blanket, pulled on boots, taking particular care with the one that had the loose sole.

Before the sun swam its way out of the river fog he and Abner Wilfong bought the necessary supplies. Charlie had always been afraid of guns, long before the villainous Corpal Slink winged him. Still, on the advice of a desiccated old man in greasy buckskins, he bought one of the new Spencer repeating rifles and a supply of .56–.56 metal-cased cartridges.

"You listen to what Mr. Coogan says, Charlie," Abner Wilfong admonished him. "He's took a dozen or more wagon trains out to Oregon and Californy and never lost nobody."

"Except them that died of the cholera," Ike Coogan corrected. "No, you get out in the Platte Valley and you got Pawnees to the north and Cheyennes to the south. When they ain't fighting each other, they're hoorawing wagon trains. Sometimes it's like getting caught between the anvil and the hammer. You take my advice, young feller, and buy the Spencer. It's only twenty-eight dollars, and you can load it of a Sunday and it'll shoot all week!"

Coogan was the dirtiest man Charlie had ever seen. Crusts of dirt ringed his wrists and the bare ankles that disappeared into beaded moccasins. He also had a powerful smell which Charlie quickly moved upwind of. "Thank you, sir," he said politely. "I guess you'd know." He had seven dollars left.

After the noon ferry crossing, they traveled over the luxuriant grass across the plains. With the grass had come wild flowers. The Kansas prairies, rolling in soft pillowy mounds, were as lovely as a woman's breasts. Even Abner Wilfong's mules seemed happy to leave the brawling activity of St. Joe and leaned into the harness. Betsy, Sarah, and Grandma Wilfong rode on the high seat, Grandma minding the reins and the brake while Abner and Charlie walked beside the mules. They were near the end of the file of thirty or more wagons. Riding a speckled pony with a queer high-backed saddle, Ike Coogan trotted along the train from time to time.

"Everything fine, Abner?" he asked.

"Yes, sir, Mr. Coogan! Fine as frog hair!"

However, roiling black clouds rose in the west. In late afternoon a chill wind blew, rippling the grass. Unprepared for the variable nature of Kansas weather, Abner and Charlie ran for the wagon as the sky exploded with forked bolts of lightning. Wind lashed torrents of rain that stung like angry bees. The women retreated into the boxes and bales and trunks and sacks that filled the wagon bed while Abner and Charlie huddled together on the high seat.

"Stupid mules!" Abner shouted, sawing at the reins. "Skeered of a little weather! Ho, there — you, Jupiter — behave yourself!"

Jupiter reared and brayed long and loud as a stroke of fire hit a bush near them. The bush disappeared in a blue-white flash, leaving only a smoking skeleton.

146

Charlie wiped rain-blinded eyes. "That was close!"

"Never hits twice in the same place, I heard," Abner said in a shaky voice.

They could hardly make out the wagons ahead in the wind-driven sheets of rain. The Wilfong women were singing a hymn. Charlie joined fervently in the chorus:

Rock of ages, cleft for me.
Let me hide myself in thee!

There was no place to hide. The air smelled like sulphur and brimstone. Surely the Old Gentleman would not immolate this nice Wilfong family just to get at Charlie Callaway! Anyway, Charlie was singing the tenor part as fervently as he knew how. Whether this had any celestial effect he did not know, but as quickly as it came the storm rolled off to the east, leaving a waning orange sun wreathed in scattered streamers of cloud. Slanting rays lit the wet grass so that the plain seemed spangled with diamonds. Birds reappeared, soaring high in the fresh-washed sky, and a family of quail scuttled away from their wheels. To his surprise Charlie found that small Betsy had been sitting beside him for some time, hand slipped into his.

"Oh, my!" she marveled. "Ain't it pretty!"

Ike Coogan, riding along the train, issued instructions for the night's camp near a gravelly brook, now washed clean and icy from the rain. Following his hand signals, the train looped into a circle with such precision that the last wagon neatly filled the gap in the ring. Soon fires blazed, lamps were lit, men gathered in

147

small groups discussing the storm while the women cooked supper. The Wilfongs' wagon canvas had been saturated with linseed oil in an effort to waterproof it, but still leaked badly. Charlie and Abner, waiting to be fed, sopped up the water with rags and spread things out to dry.

"Guess Bets kind of took a shine to you," Grandma Wilfong said to Charlie. "Well, vittles is ready, men! Wash up!"

After supper Charlie played his sweet potato while a silent ring of listeners came from the other wagons.

"I'm that wet from the rain I'd like to warm meself with a little jig!" a pug-nosed man said. "Friend, do you know 'The Wee Cooper of Fife'?"

"I sure do," Charlie said.

While he tootled the Irishman did a heel-and-toe dance, arms hanging straight at his side. A red-haired girl sang the words in a clear soprano:

> *There was a cooper lived in Fife,*
> *Nickety, nackety, noo, noo noo.*
> *And he had got him a gentle wife*
> *Hey, Willie O'Daugherty, nackety noo!*

The song went on endlessly, but the Irishman was tireless.

> *She wouldna card, she wouldna spin*
> *For the shamin' of her gentle kin.*
> *The cooper went to his wee shack*
> *And put a sheepskin across her back.*

148

I wouldna thrash ye for your gentle kin
But I would thrash my ain sheepskin!

There was a roar of laughter, applause. Someone brought a fiddle, and a Jew's harp twanged in a droning bass. In response to the clamor the impromptu orchestra played on: "The Gray Goose," "Skip to My Lou," and "Old Blue." Gradually the mood of the listeners changed. When Charlie played "Sourwood Mountain" a few of the women dabbed at their eyes, remembering homes and hearth, relatives and friends left behind. Gradually the crowd slipped off to rest against the hard day ahead. In the pale light of the moon Sarah Wilfong gently pulled Betsy away from Charlie.

"Come, dear! It's time for bed."

"I don't want to go, Mama."

"But you must!"

Betsy threw her arms about Charlie and kissed him on the cheek. "Will you play your potato again tomorrow, Mr. Callaway?"

"I will," he said. "Forever and forever, if you want me to, Betsy!"

When they were gone Abner Wilfong knocked out his pipe. "Poor little fatherless tyke," he murmured.

"I guess I'm not exactly the father type," Charlie said, putting away the sweet potato, "but maybe I can fill in till we get to Sacramento."

It did not take long for the novelty and excitement of the trip to wear off. Children began to get cranky, men were weary of the endless prairie, women grew tired of cooking with buffalo chips, the only fuel available. A few families had small iron cooking stoves but the chips would not burn in them. The only remedy was to build a fire outside and constantly tend the cooking pots. As they traveled, the train spread out longer and longer. One wagon threw a tire, another's oxen stampeded when approached by coyotes, a third wagon pulled out to let an old lady breathe her last, free of the endless rolling and pitching. Charlie pulled a few teeth. As the only man in the train with any medical experience, he set two broken arms and sewed up a gash in a foot caused by an inexpertly swung axe. Ike Coogan rode back and forth along the straggling column in his high-backed Sioux saddle, exhorting the wagons to close up. At nightly community meetings he emphasized the need to stay together.

"Ain't nothing much around here but Kanza tribe," he said, "and they don't bother no one 'less'n they're drunk. But soon we'll be in genuine one-hundred-proof-hostile country — lift-your-hair country — and we got to have *discipline!*"

Two weeks out of St. Joe they reached the Big Blue, a tributary of the Kansas River, where they would ford the wagons. The Big Blue was high with recent rains. While they waited, Betsy was Charlie's constant companion.

At her request he held lengthy conversations with her dolls, Mandy and Everett Wilfong, and sipped imaginary tea from a tiny cup. He taught her how to play Old Sledge and delighted her with card tricks using a tattered deck, taking the ace of diamonds from her ear, making a poker hand vanish in midair, pulling the very card she had chosen out of the deck after she had slipped it in at random.

"You *are* smart, Mr. Callaway!"

He shook his head. "Not very, Betsy. Just — well, maybe *clever*."

"Will you play your potato, please? Mandy does so like to hear 'The Irish Washerwoman'!"

The delay at Alcove Springs was longer than expected and there was some worry about dwindling food supplies. A few led cows behind their wagons, and so had a source of fresh milk. Extra milk hung in a bucket beneath the wagon quickly turned into butter. Eggs had been packed in barrels of cornmeal; as the eggs were used up, the meal was baked into cakes. Slabs of smoked bacon kept well as long as they were protected against the heat of the plains, which was sometimes difficult. While there was no immediate problem, a troop of hunters was organized to bring back fresh meat; antelope were plentiful, and, though buffalo had been pretty well hunted out, Charlie killed a huge cow at two hundred yards range with his Spencer rifle, giving him a reputation for marksmanship he did not entirely deserve.

Finally fording the Big Blue, the train pressed on, compact and short-coupled at least for the moment. It was well into June when they reached the infamous Platte River, which, for the most part, this late in the season, was only a broad band of flowing silt. Ike Coogan sarcastically described it as "running near the top of the ground." Someone else said it "looked a mile wide and an inch deep." At a distance of about three miles on either side of the river the land rose in sandstone cliffs. Noticing the burned timber on the sandy islands, Abner Wilfong asked Ike Coogan about them.

"Burned off by Injuns to ketch small game," Ike said. "This here is the beginning of Injun country. So all be keerful, you hear me?"

Now the valley of the Platte began to tilt sharply upward. The wagons toiled and struggled toward the sandstone ridges. Beyond, there was a sudden drop toward the valley of the North Platte, where it was necessary to "chain" the wagons down the slope by snubbing ropes around rocks, trees, anything that would give a purchase. Three wagons broke loose and tumbled to the bottom in a shower of splinters, disgorging family portraits, mahogany bureaus, mattresses, pots and pans. The unfortunate families were forced to double up with others.

After the sandy banks of the North Platte, the rising altitude brought steadily colder nights. Far off on the horizon loomed the snow-patched Laramie Mountains. Closer by, at various points along the trail, they saw the four-hundred-foot-high heap of rock and clay that someone had dubbed the Court House because of its fancied resemblance to a municipal building in St. Louis. Fourteen miles farther was Chimney Rock, thrusting its giant bulk five hundred feet into the air. At a nooning one man walked around it at the base, coming back with the report that it took an even ten thousand and forty steps to encircle it.

152

"Damn fool!" Ike Coogan grumbled. "Better save his strength for what's coming! Beyond Fort Laramie — that's where the real rough going starts!"

So far they had only seen roving bands of Indians, who had kept well at a distance. A few — tall, bandy-legged men with painted faces and feathers in their hair — had come warily into camp to trade furs for tobacco, coffee, and sugar. "Sioux," Ike said. "Part of Turkey Leg's people."

"Are they — are they dangerous?" Sarah Wilfong asked.

"Out here, any Injun's dangerous! Don't turn your back on any of 'em!"

Early in July the train was still several days short of Fort Laramie. Much of the immigrants' supplies had been used up already, along with the strength of the mules and patient oxen. It was discouraging to realize that they were only about a third of the way to California — or Oregon, for those who would split off at Fort Hall on the Raft River. Too, there were more frequent brushes with roving bands of Sioux and Cheyenne. The tribes had been infuriated by a recent defeat at the hands of the U.S. cavalry and were attempting to close off the wagon roads west. More and more of the painted warriors were seen in ever-larger bands. They dogged the wagons, rode a mile or so out on the flanks, and even appeared on the trail ahead, but the size of the train had so far intimidated them.

Ike Coogan, sharing a cup of fast-dwindling coffee with the Wilfongs, was not optimistic. "They got something on their minds," he said, "and it ain't jolly!

153

Soon's they gather up enough braves, they'll probable try to rush us afore we get to Fort Laramie. Keep an eye peeled, folks!"

Little Betsy burrowed deeper into the comforting crook of her mother's arm, blue eyes wide, a finger in her mouth.

"Don't want to skeer anyone needless," Ike said, draining the cup and putting it down. "Still, facts is facts! Guess no one starts out on a excursion like this without knowing what kin happen."

They were traversing a rocky pass, a weathered wilderness of gulches, needlelike spires, and shelflike parapets, when the combined Indian forces struck. The passage had been difficult, and all the men in the train turned out to push, drag, and haul individual wagons to the summit. The train was thus immobilized and in no condition to repel an assault. Ike Coogan had sent scouts out on the ridges, scanning the boulder-strewn slope, but the Sioux and the Cheyenne slipped around them. Charlie's first knowledge of the attack was when a feathered arrow ripped into the tight-stretched canvas of the wagon top, tearing a gaping hole. Another arrow thunked into the grease bucket dangling from the rear axle. There were cries of alarm as men scurried to pick up weapons while others herded women and children under the wagons. Charlie dropped the iron bar he had been using to pry a Wilfong wagon wheel loose and picked up his rifle.

"Get under the wagon!" Abner Wilfong shouted. "You, Sarah, and Ma!" He looked around in bewilderment. "Where's Bets?"

Sarah Wilfong screamed, choked it off with a clenched fist to her mouth. "Pa, she was playing — over there!" She pointed to a rocky hollow near the trail. "She took her dolls and —"

Abner, carrying his shotgun, started to run toward the hollow, but Charlie grabbed his coat and pulled him back. "Stay here! The women need you!"

"But —"

"Go! Get them out of the line of fire!" As he spoke a ball whizzed past his ear and spattered on a nearby rock, the shower of lead nearly blinding him. More arrows drove deep into the wagon bed, and he heard the chilling war whoop of the attackers. Digging at his eyes, he ran low over the littered slope, stumbling and falling, picking himself up to run again. An arrow hit the heel of a boot already in bad shape, and he felt a sting. Calling "Bets! Where are you?" he broke off the shaft of the arrow and hobbled forward.

"Bets! Betsy! For God's sake, where are you?"

Above him the Indians were sneaking down through the rocks, dodging from cover to loose a shower of lances, arrows, and musket fire. Under Ike Coogan's direction the men had established a defensive position behind the wagons.

"Bets! Call out to me, child! Where are you?"

He found her among her dolls, crouched in a rocky nest, small hand jammed into her mouth to muffle her sobs.

"Mr. Callaway! I — I was so afraid!"

He dropped down beside her. "Don't worry, Bets. It's going to be all right!" Carefully he poked his head

155

above the rim of rocks. "Look, now! You can't stay here! I — I'm going to shoot a lot of bullets out there to keep their heads down and —"

"The Indians?"

"Yes, the Indians." He scanned the hundred yards or so between them and the Wilfong wagon. "I want you to be brave, Betsy. Will you be brave?"

Tear-streaked face sober, she nodded.

"Are you a fast runner?"

"Yes."

A bullet spanged off a nearby ledge. For a moment Charlie saw a painted face stare at him, then vanish as he brought up the barrel of the Spencer.

"If you run fast, behind that line of rocks, you're small enough to be hidden. I want you to run to the wagon while I —" Cover you, he thought. That wouldn't mean anything to this small girl. "Imagine you're in a race," he said, "and you're going to get a big gold star, like at school, when you win."

"But my dolls —"

He swallowed hard. "I'll — I'll bring them when I come."

She shook her head. "I want to be here with you, Mr. Callaway. I — I feel better with you." She clung to him, weeping again.

"You can't!" he cried, cringing with her in his arms as their unseen antagonist fired again. This time the report sounded nearer; Charlie almost felt the muzzle blast. "Bets, you've got to go! Quick now!"

When she still clung to him he pushed her roughly away. "Bets, you're being a bad little girl! I don't like you anymore!" God help me! he thought. But I have to do it! He slapped her harder than he had meant to. One hand to her cheek, she drew away from him, blue eyes unbelieving.

"Now go!" he shouted. "Go away, quick! Run to the wagon! I — I don't like you anymore!"

She gave him a last hurt look and ran toward the safety of the wagons, bounding like a deer, winding in and out of the screen of rocks. Above the rattle of gunfire, the war whoops, the shouts from the beleaguered defenders of the wagon train, he heard her sobs.

"It was for the best," he told the Old Gentleman. "I never did a whole lot I was proud of, but this time I expect you've got to let me in and not obfuscate things with a lot of chin music!"

Cautiously he peeked over the rocky ledge, raising the rifle. At the same time he felt something sharp jab his ribs. Rolling over, he found himself confronted by a ring of painted faces. Lying sheltered among the rocks, the Indians grinned evilly. The one with the lance prodded him again. Another man wearing a furry cap ornamented with buffalo horns raised a musket and took a bead on Charlie Callaway's face.

"I won't be long," Charlie told the Old Gentleman. "Unless —"

Smiling a tight-lipped smile, he laid down the Spencer and reached into his pocket. For a moment he expected to have his head blown off; Buffalo Horn's finger tightened on the trigger and the stocky short-necked man with the lance drew it back to gather strength for the deadly thrust. Charlie took out the dog-eared deck of Steamboat cards.

"Now," he said, his voice quavering, "if you gentlemen will gather round and give me your attention, I'll show you a few amazing card tricks!"

CHAPTER
NINE

Little Pete, accompanied by *boo how doy* in black coats and flat-brimmed hats, sauntered into the Christian Mission to the Chinese in Brooklyn Alley. Lorna and old Dah Pah Tsin were boiling rice and wilted vegetables in a copper pot. Lorna looked up to see the King of the Tongs in the doorway — squat and stylish in suit of English cut and a bowler hat contrasting oddly with the pigtail.

"You get out, Missy Bascomb," he said, bowing.

Lorna, tired and weary, straightened, pushed back a vagrant lock of hair. "What?"

Little Pete sidled forward, beaming. The *boo how doy* took up positions on each side of the doorway. One went outside and scanned the teeming streets for homicidal rivals to Little Pete's throne.

"I say you get out from here!" A hand heavy with rings waved negligently about, taking in the shabby rooms, the broken windows, the board floor that was split and rotting. "I own building! I need!"

Dah Pah Tsin spat meaningfully into a corner. Loi San, the small discarded prostitute who had been peeling carrots, averted her face and fled.

"You need this building? For what, pray?"

Little Pete smiled again. This time there was menace in the creasing of the broad features. "You not ask why! I need! My business!"

Lorna forced her voice to sound casual.

"Mr. Pete, this effort here — the mission — is the only agency in Little China relieving the misery of your poor and oppressed people! Surely you cannot deny us this small building! We have tried to pay the rent monthly and are only a little behind. Please, can you not —"

"You cause trouble!"

"Trouble?"

Little Pete pointed a silver-mounted walking stick at her. "You and your uncle! Cause trouble! Make Chinese people against me! They talk to you, don't do what I say no more! They think they no belong to Little Pete no more — belong to —" The walking stick swung, pointing to the chromo of Jesus Christ on the wall. "Think they belong *him!*" He shook his head violently, rapped the cane on the floor.

"But —"

"No more talk!" He turned away, nodded to the *boo how doy*, who formed a protective phalanx about him. Then he turned, apparently having a new thought. "Unless —"

Lorna stood her ground. "Unless — what?"

He sidled near; she smelled opium, sweat. "White men like China girl!" He whispered the words. "China man like white girl, too, maybe!"

"What — what are you saying?"

160

"You love China people so much, lady! You help them lot more, you have money, things, whole big place to help, if you be nice."

"Nice!" One hand was on her throat, and her voice trembled.

"Yes, missy. Be nice!"

She managed to steady her voice. "You are insulting!"

The slanted eyes narrowed; Little Pete's moon-bland face hardened into stone. "So you lose chance, lady!" One week I give you! No more! Everything and all people be out of here in one week! Then I tear down building and put up new Palace of Delight!" He waved the walking stick mockingly in farewell. "Business good with me! Business bad with you! Good-bye, missy!"

When he had gone, little Loi San emerged from a closet, frightened. Under Lorna Bascomb's ministrations the child had gained weight and often smiled. The sores on her face and arms had healed. "What do now?" she asked in anguished tones.

Lorna's voice was shaky but determined. "Why, we will fight on, of course!"

Sweat bathing him in an icy dew, Charlie fanned the cards into a perfect circle. "Remarkable, eh? Notice the precision — each card separated from the next by exactly six degrees!" He pushed the fanned deck into the face of No Neck, who drew back, muttering. "Here, sir — take a card, any card! No? Well, then —" He flipped the ace of spades high into the air. It soared like a bird, then returned to his hand in a fair simulation of

161

an Australian boomerang. Seeing the savage faces follow the flight of the ace, he flung more cards into the air until they looked like a flight of white doves. "Pretty good, eh? The Great Bordoni never did it any better on the stage!"

No Neck glanced up the hill where the battle of the wagon train was going on with diminished activity. Ike Coogan, Charlie remembered, said that Indians never mounted a sustained battle. They hit hard and quick, then disappeared.

"Now here's another one that will surprise and amaze you!" he announced desperately, gathering up the cards. "I will put the whole deck in my ear, card by card, and then make it mysteriously reappear. Watch, fellow Americans!"

Some of the warriors, having broken off the battle, were sliding down the rocky slope and gesturing to Charlie's captors to join them as they disappeared into a cactus-studded canyon. No Neck made a guttural sound, like the coughing grunt Charlie had once heard a circus bear make. He raised his lance for a final thrust into Charlie's giblets. Frantically Charlie dropped the cards into his pocket, and took out the ocarina, his sweet potato. Music hath charms to soothe the savage beast! he thought. Or was it the savage breast? No matter, now! "For a grand finale," he announced, stepping lively to offer a moving target, "I will favor you with a selection of patriotic melodies!" It could well be the grand finale — his own.

"'Columbia, the Gem of the Ocean,'" he announced. When he put the sweet potato to his lips he found his mouth so dry he could hardly manage a pucker; a shrill gasp was all that came out. "I'll throw in a jig at the same time," he offered, finally starting to tootle on the instrument. At the same time, to No Neck's considerable annoyance, he danced about in panic. Frantically he looked up the hill, hoping the immigrants would rush to rescue him; no one came. Buffalo Horn stared, apparently thinking Charlie crazy. Perhaps he *was* crazy; crazy with fear.

"*Hopo!*" Buffalo Horn said suddenly, pushing aside No Neck's lance. Charlie didn't know what *hopo* meant, but he was glad to be rid of the deadly lance. Maybe *hopo* was a form of address.

Sweating, he bowed to Buffalo Horn. "*Hopo*, yourself!"

Buffalo Horn shoved him so that he almost fell and pointed to the mouth of the rocky canyon. Charlie gave a last despairing look up the slope. His companions of the wagon train must be there, searching the slopes, perhaps for Charlie Callaway; a musket ball spanged off a flat ledge and whickered away down the canyon. Buffalo Horn gave him another push, gesturing toward the canyon.

"Charlie! Charlie Callaway!" He heard a female voice, raised high; Sarah Wilfong was calling. He thought also he heard another voice, a child's beseeching wail. "Mr. Callaway! Where are you?" That would be little Bets. But the Sioux devils were taking him away as a captive. He would never again see Abner and Grandma Wilfong, never see little Bets — never even see Lorna Bascomb.

Moving fast, they prodded him through a narrow defile till they came to where they had tied their horses. The rest of the Sioux were there. One brave had a furry blood-dripping thing tucked in his belt. Charlie recognized it as a scalp, and his stomach became queasy. It looked like the rich thatch of the pug-nosed Irishman who had done the heel-and-toe dance that first night out from St. Joe. He slumped on a sun-warm rock but Buffalo Horn dragged him to his feet, pointing out a piebald pony with a high-backed wooden saddle. "Up!" he growled. "Up!" Buffalo Horn apparently knew a few words of English.

"Listen," Charlie pleaded. "This is all a mistake! I *like* Indians! Once I gave a dollar to the Friends of the Indian Association in Washington, D.C. Thank you very much, but if the fun is over, I'll just sashay back and join my pals."

Impatient, Buffalo Horn pricked Charlie's ribs with a feather-hafted knife drawn from a leather sheath.

"All right," Charlie wheezed. Legs trembling, he managed to clamber into the saddle. Buffalo Horn and the rest of the party mounted, and the war party rode deep into the recesses of the canyon. He hoped little Bets would find her precious dolls.

It was July, and the narrow canyon was a bake-oven. A dozen Sioux rode ahead, another dozen behind. No Neck was on one side and Buffalo Horn on the other. They kept a watchful eye on him. He thought briefly of escape, driving heels into the pony's ribs and taking a gambler's chance of galloping up the canyon wall to freedom. But he was no horseman; the only thing that kept him on the painted pony was the high-backed saddle. He sweated, prayed, gave thanks that the glittering lance had not yet pierced his vitals. He was alive. While Charlie Callaway was alive, he would think of something. So far he always had.

The sun was low in the west when they broke out to a grassy valley. The Sioux appeared to be glad the day's journey had ended. They joked and laughed, probably bragging about the victorious raid.

"Nothing funny about it, nothing at all!" Charlie muttered between clenched teeth.

Buffalo Horn grabbed his sweat-sodden shirt. "You say — what?"

"Just commenting on the lovely view," Charlie explained. "Green grass, water —" He pointed to a winding stream in the distance. "Nice spot to rest, I should think."

The war party hobbled horses, started a fire, took out leathery strings of meat and chewed them, ignoring Charlie. Afterward, they bound him hand and foot and rolled him against a tree as one rolls a log. Stars began to pinprick the velvet sky. After a while the braves slept, rolled in blankets, feet to the dying fire. A lone sentinel squatted on a rock jutting out from the thick grass. Unable to sleep, Charlie listened to the night sounds — the whickering and shuffling of the ponies' unshod hoofs, the purling of the little stream, the gentle movement of a night breeze across the grass. He fixed his gaze on a twinkling star. Venus, perhaps? Symbol of love? Was that same planet looking down on Lorna Bascomb, so far away on the western ocean? "Tell her, star," he whispered, "that I always loved her! I always will, even when I am

165

being roasted alive by these savage heathen!" After a while he slept.

Someone jabbed him in the ribs. He looked up to see No Neck grinning evilly. In the east was only a faint glimmer of dawn. Still bound, he managed to stagger to his knees. For amusement, No Neck knocked him down again. Still grinning, he dragged Charlie to his feet and untied him. "*Hopo*," he said again.

Let's go, Charlie thought. That was what it must mean.

"*Hopo*," he wearily agreed, and got back on the painted horse again, slumping in the painted wooden cradle.

In mid-morning the Sioux came finally to their camp, a cluster of lodges in a shallow rocky bowl. A mountain stream burbled through the bowl to fall in a silvery cascade to the plains below. Women and children crowded around the returning warriors. They gazed curiously at Charlie. One small boy, more daring than the rest, ran out and tugged at Charlie's ragged pants leg, then dashed back to the safety of his mothers skirts.

In the center of the ring of lodges was one much larger, painted with stars and moons and jagged streaks of red and yellow and black. Buffalo Horn signaled Charlie to dismount, then herded him to the big lodge, where he scratched politely at the doorflap. In response to a murmur from within, he pushed Charlie through the doorway.

Inside it was dark and gloomy in spite of the brilliant morning sunshine. The interior smelled of wood smoke; a tin pot of coffee bubbled on a small fire. It took

Charlie some time to regain his sight, make out a small wizened figure sitting on an Army ammunition chest covered with a fur robe. Naked except for a breechclout and a fur hat decorated with feathers, the old man wore a necklace of animal claws around his withered neck. Pushing Charlie forward, Buffalo Horn went into a long discourse in a Sioux gabble, reinforcing his account by quick hand gestures.

Silently the old man — probably the high chief — listened, working toothless gums. From time to time he sipped at a crockery cup of coffee.

"Eh?" Charlie, lost in a dismal contemplation of his fate, jumped. "What?"

Buffalo Horn made a gesture that was unmistakable, riffling an imaginary pack of playing cards and dealing them out. "Make — tricks!"

Feeling a prickle of hope, Charlie took out his dog-eared deck. Too weary and dejected to keep up a line of patter, he only went through the motions, Still, he seemed to catch the old man's interest. Warming to the task, he began to instill life into the tattered pasteboards, causing them to fly here and there, to emerge at odd places, to be plucked from Buffalo Horn's beaded leather vest.

"*Hau!*" the old man exclaimed.

Daring, Charlie finally approached the chief. Buffalo Horn, nervous, pulled at him in alarm, but Charlie shook him off. What did he have to lose anyway but his life? His fingers moved so fast that the cards blurred; suddenly the whole deck vanished. Under the wrinkled lids the chief's eyes grew wide. Like a child he felt

167

through Charlie's pockets, ran his hand about, seeking the vanished cards. He muttered something that must have meant "Where did they go?"

With a flourish Charlie snatched off the old man's fur hat and showed him the deck of cards within. There was a sharp intake of breath; the chief put a hand over his mouth. "*Wakan!*" he murmured. "*Wakan!*"

Charlie did not know until later what that word meant. *Wakan* was the Sioux word used to describe something magic, possibly even connected with the pantheon of Sioux gods. At any rate, they gave him a tepee of his own, together with a lissome Sioux maid named Red Leaf who was the granddaughter of old Turkey Leg, chief of as murderous a band of Sioux warriors as ever attacked a wagon train.

Sitting cross-legged near the fire, he spooned meat stew from a wooden bowl, vaguely uncomfortable at Red Leaf's presence. For a female she was tall and long-limbed, her hair a sleek and shining black, the face a delicate oval in which dark eyes made luminous pools. As usual, she served him first. In fact, he never knew when Red Leaf ate, or if she did. As always she sat near him, legs modestly to one side, eyes averted as her lord and master supped.

So far as Charlie Callaway knew she understood no word of English, but he felt constrained to speak anyway.

"You know," he said, gesturing with the horn spoon, "this is a very peculiar situation for me! I am practically engaged to a very nice lady out in San Francisco and it doesn't seem right for a nubile young female like you to be sleeping in the same tent with me."

Red Leaf smiled, went on combing her hair.

"Now I'm a normal man, with a normal man's instincts." He swallowed hard when she rose, her buckskin skirt falling away to show a firm young thigh; her skin was not so much coppery as flushed with a rosy tint. "I guess what I mean — I'd just as soon you slept outside. Or maybe I'll sleep outside. At any rate, we ought not sleep together."

When she knelt beside him to pour coffee into his cup, he groaned. Who was it in the Bible who was subjected to agonizing fleshly temptations? Whoever he was, he was probably a saint. Charlie Callaway was no saint.

Still, he could not complain. Old Turkey Leg liked him, calling him frequently to the big lodge. Charlie did card tricks, played the sweet potato, declaimed passages from Shakespeare with dramatic gestures to help the old man while away an enfeebled life. In a stew of gestures and the gabbling Sioux language mingled with a few words of English, they got along. Buffalo Horn, the tribe's medicine man, became jealous of Charlie's influence, however, and Buffalo Horn seemed to be a powerful and important man.

Turkey's Leg's favorite was the great speech in *Henry V*, act III. For the tenth or eleventh time Charlie recited it, striding about the dimlit smoky lodge and lending the words his best effort, although he was getting rather tired of Henry:

Once more unto the breach, dear friends, once more;
Or close up the wall with our English dead!
In peace there's nothing so becomes a man
As modest stillness and humility:
But when the blast of war blows in our ears —

This morning the old man seemed unresponsive, almost dejected. When a squaw brought him a bowl of boiled roots mashed into a pulp he threw the bowl at her, scowling.

— Then imitate the action of the tiger;
Stiffen up the sinews, summon up the blood,
Disguise fair nature —

Charlie was a quick study and had already picked up a few Sioux words, some of the eloquent gestures. Turkey Leg had no teeth, and the old man longed for solid food — meat, red meat. He made Charlie understand that lack of red meat was the reason for his infirmities.

Charlie nodded in sympathy. "Meat — yes. Meat is good!" Turkey Leg sighed; his head dropped on his meager chest. Apparently he dozed, and Charlie silently slipped from the lodge. Poor old fellow!

Poor old fellow! He rebuked himself. Turkey Leg's band of Sioux was a savage wall raised against legitimate migration across the plains! How could anyone be sorry for a Sioux? Almost daily their war parties set out to harass wagon trains, steal horses, skirmish with the outnumbered U.S. cavalry. No, he

170

would not be sorry! Going back to his lodge, he saw Buffalo Horn squatting in front of his tepee. The medicine man eyed Charlie Callaway malevolently and continued honing a knife on a stone. Charlie still felt an evil eye on his back and turned. Buffalo Horn was waving a feather-tipped wand at him, chanting a cabalistic curse.

"I'm not scared, you old bastard!" Charlie muttered. Nevertheless, he felt uneasy.

The days wore on. He thought of escape but was watched constantly. Where would he go? How would he survive in this strange land — harsh desert and rugged mountains, with only a few scattered grassy valleys? Not on foot, certainly, and he was afraid of horses; they bit. As autumn approached he sighed and endured, watching the trees turn color, seeing the glaze of frost on the grass, aware the midday sun was losing its warmth and dropping lower in the sky.

He had finally given in to Red Leaf's blandishments. She was utterly without shame, making him aware of sensual feelings he did not know were possible. Recalling the whores he had known, along with more legitimate conquests when he was on the riverboats, he thought them rather inconsequential compared to the Sioux compendium of delights.

Lying with her in the lodge while a cold wind rippled the skins, he felt deliciously content. While he lay naked with her among the fur robes, she stroked him with a gentle hand.

"Happy?" she asked. It was one of the words he had taught her.

"Yes, happy." Still, *he* was not happy. Lorna Bascomb's face came between them, and then Red Leaf was hurt that he seemed reserved, far away. Still, what could he do? He was a captive, and perhaps his very existence depended on adherence to their way of life. When in Rome —

Eyes sad, she drew away. He pulled her to him again. "It's nothing," he whispered. "*Iktomi* is on my back."

She understood. *Iktomi* was the trickster god, the god who caused trouble, harassed people, played tricks on them. *Iktomi* had played a trick on Charlie Callaway, all right.

Red Leaf was not his only concern. Turkey Leg became increasingly annoyed at Charlie, tired of Shakespeare and the tootling of Charlie's sweet potato. Also, the old man discovered the secrets of some of Charlie's card tricks and lost interest. But there was another factor. Red Leaf made him understand that Buffalo Horn was telling lies about him to Turkey Leg, trying to discredit him. Weeping, she clung to Charlie, afraid her grandfather might withdraw his favor. The Sioux might cut his throat then, as a nuisance, or drive him from the camp to die in the mountains. Already snow capped the highest peaks, and the tepees, at a lower elevation, were sometimes dusted with the white stuff at dawn.

"Now don't you worry," Charlie soothed her. "I can take care of myself!"

In a mist of new downfall he went to the big lodge to scratch at the doorflap. When he entered he found Buffalo Horn squatting at the foot of the dais, smoking a pipe with Turkey Leg. They looked on him with disfavor. Again Buffalo Horn shook the tasseled wand and muttered a curse. Turkey Leg's old eyes were hard and distant.

"Teeth!" Charlie announced, tapping his own. "You." He pointed to Turkey Leg. "You. Teeth. I make for you."

They stared.

"I know you don't understand all I'm saying, but I used to be a dentist." Again he tapped his teeth. "Me. Doctor. Fix teeth!"

Buffalo Horn rose, circled Charlie, muttering imprecations. Charlie disregarded him.

"I — make — you — teeth," he said slowly. "You — eat meat — again."

Capering about, Buffalo Horn started to howl like an animal in an effort to drown out Charlie's words. Old Turkey Leg silenced him with a harsh Sioux expletive and the medicine man squatted sulkily.

"Teeth?" Turkey Leg asked. "Me?"

"Yes, you! I can make teeth! You can eat meat again — ribs, liver, marrow bones, fat rump! You can eat all of it, be young and strong again!" In a way he had told a lie — the old man would never be young — but Charlie Callaway was fighting for his life.

Turkey Leg sank back on the dais. Puffing his pipe, he eyed Charlie. Buffalo Horn muttered something but the old man paid him no attention.

"Teeth," he murmured. He ran a bony finger about his shrunken gums, "You — make — teeth?"

"Yes, God damn it! I sure as hell make teeth, fine teeth! I've done it lots of times! Trust me, just trust me!"

"Trust?" The old man was puzzled by the word.

Charlie held up a hand, swearing to the Sioux gods or any others who might be around. "I — make — you — teeth!"

Turkey Leg was doubtful; Charlie saw it in his eyes. Only the Sioux gods could do miracles, and the old man had beseeched the gods without success. Still —

Finally Turkey Leg nodded, making the sign for "agree," two forefingers held together. Our minds run the same way.

Buffalo Horn was still arguing with Turkey Leg when Charlie hurried from the lodge. Charlie didn't care. He knew he had convinced Turkey Leg, at least for the present. He had already lost two sets of dentist's tools and had none of the molds and casts and adhesives needed for making false teeth. Nevertheless, he would do it — somehow.

George Washington, he remembered from an old school book, had used a set of wooden teeth working against a steel spring. That was almost a hundred years ago. If a nearly medieval dentist could make George a set of teeth then, why couldn't Charlie Callaway do it now? He was clever with his hands and had graduated from a modern dental school.

Ref Leaf and her mother, a stocky bandy-legged woman with a perpetual smile, helped. To Turkey Leg's great discomfiture, Charlie made a clay cast of the old man's shrunken gums, allowing it to harden in the sun. Red Leaf brought him a collection of coyote teeth. They had been part of a medicine sack her dead father wore, but now they were sacrificed to the greater good — the chief's longing for meat, and Charlie Callaway's neck. Buffalo Woman, Red Leaf's widowed mother, mixed up a sticky compound from roots and berries and boiled animal bones which she assured them would securely anchor the coyote teeth in the wooden forms Charlie was carving to fit old Turkey Leg's mouth.

"Soon," Charlie assured Turkey Leg. "Soon — teeth!" He pantomimed, putting an imaginary buffalo rib to his own mouth and making horrendous rending noises.

"*Hau!*" the old man exclaimed, eyes hopeful.

Buffalo Horn, who seemed always to be with the chief, only glared at Charlie and shook his tasseled medicine wand. That one will be the death of me, Charlie thought, unless I succeed!

He worked day and night, scraping, boring, polishing, fitting incisors and molars into the wooden forms. The coyote teeth, apparently securely anchored, came loose overnight, and Charlie was despondent. But the whole camp knew of his attempt to give Turkey Leg teeth. No Neck's grandmother brought him a tarry-looking glue that seemed to work better. Few of the women liked Buffalo Horn; "bad," they signed. "Bad man!"

Red Leaf was always with Charlie, comforting him, feeding him, encouraging him. She brought split marrow bones, buffalo liver, dried wild potatoes and

175

wild turnips in a savory stew, precious sap from the box elder, tasting like maple syrup and delicious poured over dried plums. Kneeling besides him while he was busy with an awl, boring more holes in the forms, she murmured, "Love — you!"

Surprised, he looked up. "Eh?"

She blushed, turned her head away. Finally she said, "Love you!" again.

In the months he had been a captive he had taught Red Leaf some English words, but did not remember "love you" being among them. Perhaps he had only dreamed of Lorna Bascomb, and muttered the words in his sleep.

Pulling her hand to him, he pressed it against his bearded lips. "I love you, too," he said. "You are one fine lady, I think!" Overcome with emotion, not realizing until then how lonely, how frustrated he had been, he dropped the set of teeth and lay beside her in the enveloping warmth of the buffalo robes. The fire burned low. Outside, the wind drove sheets of icy snowflakes against the skins of the tepee. In each other's arms they were warm and content.

Suddenly Red Leaf pulled away from him, eyes wide with fright. At the sound of bugles he sat bolt upright also. Scrambling to his feet, half naked, he ran to the doorflap. In the dim afterlight of a winter sunset, further obscured by the swirling snow, bearlike forms mounted on horses galloped about the camp, riding in a circle, hemming in the startled Sioux. The bugle sounded again, a brassy jangle. From Charlie's brief

176

and unwilling stint with the U.S. Army, he knew that call; it was the cavalry "Charge!"

Already several of the lodges were burning. A trooper rode directly at Charlie, swinging a saber. He ducked, and the horse thundered on. Another trooper carrying a torch systematically set fire to the lodges; stored ammunition popped like firecrackers. The air was thick with snow, smoke, the thud of hoofs, the victorious shouts of the troopers, along with the death songs of the few warriors who had managed to snatch up arms and make a brief fight before being ridden down, sabered, or shot to death.

Snatching open the doorflap, Charlie cried out to Red Leaf. "Run!" When she hesitated he grabbed her, dragged her through the doorway and into the swirling snow. "Run! Get away! They're burning the camp!" He looked wildly around. "They're killing everyone — women and children too! Run, God damn it!"

Not until later did he consider the bearlike troopers rescuers. Filled with rage, he dragged a soldier from his mount and wrestled him into the snow. Battering the man's face, he felt the hands clutching his throat relax. Driving his knees into the cavalryman's belly, he staggered to his feet, the man's saber gripped tight. Running low, he dodged a horse, was knocked off his feet by another, and saw Buffalo Woman cowering under a raised carbine butt. With a wild yell, a cry of anger mingled with panic, he swung the saber. It did not cut through the heavy fur coat but knocked the trooper off balance. Charlie seized a dropped Colt revolver and pulled the trigger, but the cylinder was empty.

"Stop!" he yelled. "Stop it! Don't — don't —"

Red Leaf was gone, fled into the encircling rocks. Only a charred skeleton remained of Turkey Leg's big lodge. Through the blackened and flame-fringed poles Charlie saw the old man lying dead across his fur-covered dais. Turkey Leg would never get his new teeth, never know the pleasure of biting into a fat buffalo rib. Sioux bodies littered the snow, lying at odd angles and in awkward positions like discarded dolls. A half-grown youth, legs broken, crawled away like a dying animal. A trooper idly aimed his revolver at the crippled form and then stuck the weapon back in his belt, as if the youth were not worth a bullet.

"Hell, we got a white man here!" someone said in incredulous tones.

Swaying on his feet, Charlie dropped the saber, the revolver. He was sick, and slumped to his knees, retching. A burly sergeant approached him, grabbed his hair, pulled his face up. "Who the hell are you?"

It was over. He was rescued. But they were all — dead. He began to weep.

"Hey, Grover!" the sergeant called. "We got us a rare bird here! Bring over that flask of rotgut of yours!"

Over his protests they made him drink the raw whiskey. They were puzzled at his presence, but not unkind. "Although," Grover remarked, "seems to me I seen this galoot take a swing at Corporal Olson with a saber. He on our side, sarge?"

178

"We'll find out," the sergeant said, getting to his feet. "When we get back the lootenant will wool the truth out of him!"

CHAPTER
TEN

The troopers took him, bound, to Fort Laramie, where he was turned over to be interrogated by a sad-faced lieutenant with a missing arm. With a sinking feeling Charlie recognized the officer and hoped the lieutenant did not recognize him. Charlie was certainly *stroovlich*, as plump Emma Stoltzfus had once described him; he must look like a wild man in his rags pieced out with Sioux garb. But the officer was Hopkins, the lieutenant who had come down to the river that fateful day to find Charlie Callaway in the hands of Corporal Slink and his ruffians. Charlie remembered that lost arm; it had been raised high in the air, holding a saber, to give the signal to shoot him. Almost, the sparkle of sun on that saber had been his last acquaintance with this world. Now the saber was gone, the arm was gone, and Lieutenant Hopkins, lean, somber, and cadaverous as before, was asking him questions in the same flat unpleasant voice.

"I told you!" Charlie insisted. "I was with a wagon train lead by a man named Ike Coogan. I was traveling with the Wilfong family, from Circleville, Ohio. The Sioux attacked the train, and took me prisoner while I was trying to save a little girl — Betsy Wilfong. They

180

took me to their camp. Not being familiar with the territory, I didn't know where it was. But I lived with the Sioux all these months. They were kind to me, I guess, and I did card tricks that impressed them."

"You said all that," Lieutenant Hopkins grumbled.

"Well, it's true!"

Hopkins rose and went to the window. The empty sleeve twitched. Suddenly he wheeled. "What did you say your name was?"

Caught off guard, Charlie blurted, "Callaway."

"I thought you said something else before."

"No, sir." Fair caught, he murmured, "Callaway. Charles Chaney Callaway."

Inwardly he was quaking, but the name apparently meant nothing to Hopkins. He took out a cigar and Charlie hastened to strike a match for him.

"Thanks." Hopkins puffed on the stogie, eyes narrowed as he stared at Charlie. "Sergeant McElroy says some of the men saw you fighting on the Indian side."

Charlie shook his head. "No, *sir*! All it was — I was wakened out of a sound sleep, and my brains were kind of woolly. When those troopers in bearskin coats started to gallop through the camp, I didn't know *who* they were! They might have been Crows, and you know the Crows hate the Sioux."

"Crows — wearing bearskin coats?"

Charlie shrugged. "What do I know? I'm new out here. I was just protecting my life."

Hopkins tired of baiting him. Sitting down again at the desk, he searched through papers with his one hand. "Well, I guess you're telling the truth, and I'll so report to the colonel. You might be interested to know that the Coogan train reported you missing when they came through here last summer. Your story agrees with theirs."

Charlie felt as if a too tightly wound clock spring had released its tension; he was safe. Hopkins took a bottle from a drawer, poured whiskey into two cracked cups. "So you got rescued, and the Sixth Cavalry fixed old Turkey Leg's clock for good. Those Sioux will never go after another wagon train, I tell *you!*"

Charlie sipped the whiskey; Green River — good stuff. Feeling the liquor bathe his trembling stomach in warmth, he stiffened again when Hopkins asked, "Were you in the war?"

Charlie set down the cup. Lorna Bascomb said she could always tell when he was fibbing by the way he refused to look at her; he stared at Hopkins.

"Ah — yes, sir."

"What regiment?"

Again caught off guard — his reformation had lulled his former quickness of movement — he blurted the first thing that came into his mind, a remembered fragment from the days spent with the Old Order Amish family in Pennsylvania — Amos Stoltzfus and his brood. "I — I was a staff officer with A. P. Hill's Third Corps."

Hopkins frowned. "Reb, eh?"

"Yes, sir." Hastily he added. "But the war's over now. We lost, we surely did."

182

Hopkins sighed. "Yes." Staring out the window, he sipped his whiskey, face moody. Snow was falling and a brisk wind whipped the flag on its tall staff. A blue supply wagon crunched past in the ice-thickened mud and from somewhere a bugle sounded mess call — *soupy soupy soupy!* "Damn crazy thing — I lost my arm at Lynchburg when I was with Sheridan. Only a week — one damned week — before old Lee surrendered at Appomattox Court House!"

"I'm sorry," Charlie offered.

Hopkins chewed malevolently on his stogie, eyes hard and squinty. "What makes me mad is that there were so many slackers that never served a day! Draft riots in New York City, bastards buying their way out by paying someone else to do their duty! Of course, you did your job, even if it *was* on the wrong side!"

Charlie's hand shook; the whiskey in his cup spilled.

"Well, it's not important anymore." Hopkins rose; Charlie did also. "What do you plan to do now, Callaway?"

Charlie swallowed the hard lump in his throat. "I — I don't know! It's the dead of winter, and no trains coming through. I'm handy with my hands — a good mechanic. Maybe I can find something around here to pay for my bread and beans till spring."

Hopkins nodded. "Try the ordnance sergeant. He could probably use a hand. Government don't pay much for civilian help — contract employees get a dollar a day and found." He put out his left hand and Charlie grasped it. "Good luck, Callaway."

★ ★ ★

Charlie spent the winter working for Sergeant McQuigg, a profane and drunken Irishman who knew more about guns drunk than most men sober. Charlie became adept at repairing rifles; Springfields, Henrys, Enfields, Whitworths, and Spencers. He grew especially expert, meriting McQuigg's alcoholic praise for his delicate and knowledgeable way, with pistols and revolvers: the Remington, Starr, the Colt's Navy Model 1851. Often, working at the lathe or drill press, he thought how easy it would be in the ordnance shop to put together the ultimate holdout. Here he had all the tools and materials he needed, along with spare time to design and fashion the ideal holdout. But no — he was a changed man. The vicissitudes of life had burned away the dross of his former character and left him fresh and renewed. All he had to do now was wait for spring and somehow get out to San Francisco to find Lorna Bascomb.

The long winter finally showed signs of weakening its grasp on the land. Snows melted. The parade ground was a swamp, water gushed everywhere in clear rivulets. Red snowflowers poked inquiring heads through the slush, and a few geese flapped tentatively north. As flowers bloomed, so did Charlie's hopes. Soon it would be time to go. From his shop window he anxiously watched the muddy road from the Platte country; soon there would be immigrant wagons. He took out his tattered wallet and counted the money he had made during the winter as a gunsmith: seventy-six dollars. He was flush; doing good works in a Christian manner was good business.

He had, fortunately, not seen Lieutenant Hopkins again, and was grateful for that. Hopkins might remember where he had first seen Charlie Callaway. But not a chance! Charlie felt he was on a lucky streak.

In May a shabby and battered train came in from Fort Kearney on the Platte, where they had been overtaken by bad weather and forced to spend the winter. McQuigg made a deal with the farrier sergeant and in gratitude for Charlie's services gave him a nag, a bad-tempered mare blind in one eye and vicious in nature. Charlie rode with the Cooper train along the Sweetwater. Going over the Wasatch range bitter disputes broke out among the immigrants, who were largely from Kentucky and inclined to blood feuds. Charlie stayed with them to Salt Lake City, where the train broke up for good. One man was killed and three injured in a sudden outbreak of gunfire and the Mormon authorities put the rest in jail. Disgusted, Charlie joined a party of hunters. In August he came down the Humboldt River into Lake Tahoe and so, via Carson Pass, to Sacramento, once known as Sutter's Fort.

Gold had been discovered on the American River near Sacramento seventeen years before. A lot of the easy gold had been taken out, but the sprawling river town was still flushed with gold fever. Broke now, Charlie sold the spavined old nag and saddle for ten dollars. Fifty miles from San Francisco and his love, he was balked because of lack of funds! With ten dollars he could buy in to any of the numerous poker games in the tents and shanties along the river. In the flicker of candles he stood in the background, only watching. Then he turned away with a sigh. He could become a rich man right here, his only assets a deck of cards and his nimble fingers. Feeling great rectitude, he turned his back on the easy money and walked about looking for work.

The principal business activity of Sacramento seemed to be looking for gold. No one needed a mechanic or a dentist. Finally he hiked along the river bank. Gold mining was hardly the skilled labor he was capable of, consisting for the most part of shoveling gravel into the various patterns of sluice boxes in which crosswise baffles let water and sand pass while the heavier gold settled against the barriers. Each prospector seemed to have his own unique design. There were "Rockers," "Long Toms," "Big Betsys," "Lightning Boxes," and other strange devices, each of which the owner claimed to be superior to the others.

"Need a hand?" he asked a grizzled ancient shoveling gravel into a sluice box.

"Get out!" the old man said. "Sheer off, stranger!"

"But I —"

The old man picked up a shotgun and pointed it at Charlie. "This here is my claim, and I don't allow no one to set foot on it!"

Charlie tipped his battered felt hat. "That's reasonable," he agreed. "Very reasonable, sir. Now if you'll just point that thing elsewhere, I'll be on my way."

No one seemed to want him. Charlie Callaway was a penniless outcast in a strange land, and all because he had abjured gambling! It did not seem right. Weary and discouraged, he paused before a patched and dirty tent at the river's edge. It was early in the morning, the sun poking yellow streamers through the willow thickets. At the river's edge a Long Tom stood silent and unmanned.

"Anybody in there?" Charlie called.

A snore broke off in a strangled gasp.

"Sorry to rouse you out of a sound sleep," Charlie apologized, "but I'm looking for work! Got a strong back — handy with a shovel. Pull teeth, too, and fix clocks."

There was an eruption of profanity from inside the tent. Charlie quailed, drew back. He was about to flee when something stayed him. A strange smell permeated the morning air. No, it was not a smell; it was a stink. It came vaporously from the tent, like a poisonous mist. The willow leaves seemed to blanch and curl as it seeped near.

"God damn it, ain't you got no sense to come round here in the middle of the night and wake up a honest workingman that's got a broke back from shoveling gravel all the way down to Chiny?" Scratching his backside, a bearded ancient stumbled out of the shabby tent.

So that was the source of the terrible odor! Charlie stared in amazement. "Ike! Ike Coogan!"

Blearily the old man stared at him, holding up his pants with one hand while he scratched with the other.

"Who's that now, calling my name?"

Charlie came cautiously near, held out his hand. "I can't believe it! Ike Coogan!"

187

"I know who I am, damn it! Who the hell are you?"

"Charlie Callaway! Remember when the Sioux shot up your wagon train near Fort Laramie?"

Ike was doubtful. "Tell me who you was traveling with, then. My mother didn't raise no idjits! Maybe you're just trying' to jump my claim!"

Exasperated, Charlie said, "I was with the Wilfongs, damn it! Little Bets had strayed away, and when I went to find her old Turkey Leg and his Sioux jumped me and took me prisoner!"

Ike grinned. "Guess you're for true, all right! For a minute there I wasn't sure." He shook hands. "Come back from the dead, did you? Well, if that don't take the rag off'n the bush! I'll bile some coffee and there's a pot of beans left from yestiddy. Sit down, Charlie Callaway, whilst I migrate into the bushes and moves my bowels."

Over coffee and sour-tasting beans Charlie told Ike the story of his captivity and eventual rescue by the Sixth Cavalry.

"I knew old Turkey Leg," Ike mused. "He wasn't no Sunday school teacher, but then the Sioux has got their side of the argument, too. It was their land, y'see — kind of sacred, and then these white men came."

"Tell me," Charlie demanded, "how did the wagon train come out?"

"Give 'em 'bout as good as we got. They scragged Mike Moriarty — you remember the redheaded bogtrotter that danced the jig the first night out from St. Joe? Took his hair, too! Couple of the rest got winged, but nothing serious."

"Did — did little Bets find her dolls?"

Ike looked puzzled. "Dolls?"

"Abner Wilfong's little granddaughter. She had two dolls — Everett and Mandy!"

Ike shrugged. "Guess so, since I mind her playin' with a couple dolls when we got to Sacramento."

"I'm glad. She was a sweet little girl. But when did you give up guiding wagon parties, Ike?"

Ike spat eloquently. "Last winter. Got tired of nursemaiding milksops and bellyachers! Oh, it was a chore, I tell you, and they wasn't no money in it! I'm nine years older 'n God and I figgered I needed a stake for my old age. So I been scrabbling for gold." He held up a rawhide sack. "Got me over three hundred dollars of nuggets so far! It's hard work but it pays off."

"Ike," Charlie confessed, "I'm busted, clear busted. It wouldn't be my first time on the business end of a shovel. How about taking me on?"

Ike rubbed a bristled chin, sucked at toothless gums.

"I need money, Ike! I've got a girl waiting for me in San Francisco, and I've been two years trying to get there."

"Romance, eh?"

"I love her, Ike!"

"Used to have me a gal in Denver City," Ike murmured. "Prettier 'n a little fawn! She didn't take to me gallivanting around the way I did then. Oh, I was full of piss and ginger, I was!" He broke off, staring at the burbling river. Then he said, "Guess so, pardner. A dollar a day sound right to you?"

"Yes."

They shook hands.

It was back-breaking work. Charlie shoveled gravel till his hands were blistered and his back screamed with pain. Ike manipulated the rocker and occasionally spelled Charlie with the shovel. Up and down the river men toiled in the search for gold, some working at night by the glow of coal-oil lanterns. "Easier to see gold by lamplight," Ike explained. "She sparkles, like. But I got to have my sleep."

Autumn was on its way; the trees along the river began to change color. Already there was a rime of frost on the grass when they rose each morning. According to their agreement, Ike paid off regularly. Charlie already had forty-three dollars, part of it a small bonus for his hard work, which Ike appreciated. After more of the endless beans and coffee, he walked painfully out of the tent one chilly morning to pick up his shovel. By now he had gotten into the swing of it and was lean, hard, and sunburned. The hands, those skillful hands that had dealt so many aces from the bottom of the deck, were callused and horny, seeming to have lost any flexibility except to wrap themselves around the worn handle of a shovel.

The morning was quiet and sunny. Most of the gold-seekers were still rolled in their blankets, and Ike snored in the scabrous tent. Birds sang, the river sang, riffling over the bars. The air was sweet and fresh. Charlie put his foot on the shovel and pushed hard. With a practiced swing he tossed gravel into the rocker. Then, in amazement, he dropped the shovel; the worn blade had bit into a pocket of egg-shaped objects.

190

Heart pounding, he took out his jackknife and scraped a dirty lump. The first rays of the sun shone on gold, rich gold — fine gold, so soft it cut almost like butter.

"Ike!" Grabbing a handful of the nuggets he ran to the tent, shook Ike awake. "Look here! Gold! Lots of gold! Nuggets!"

Ike sat up, scrubbing his skull with his knuckles. Blinking, he peered at the objects. He bit one, then leaped from his blankets. "God damn! Sure as hell!" Frantically he searched for his pants. "Where — where —"

Charlie was gone, kneeling in the river, scrabbling about with his hands. He found more of the river-rounded things and dropped them icy-cold into his shirt. Beside him Ike labored with the shovel. Working silently, lest they wake the camp, they took out ten or more pounds of nuggets. Then the pocket ran out.

"Happens that way sometimes," Ike wheezed. "A passel of nuggets will wash down the river, get hung up on something, form a kind of little pocket, and just lay there till someone comes along and wakes 'em up! My God — look at the way they shine!"

He insisted on giving Charlie half the nuggets. "I know I took you on for a dollar a day," he said. "I *know* that, Charlie! But you found 'em, didn't you?"

"Well — yes."

"Then we share and share alike! That's only fair!"

When Charlie left, arrayed in the best gentlemen's finery the city of Sacramento could provide, he shook hands with Ike. That didn't seem like enough. Instead, to the old man's great embarrassment, he hugged Ike

191

Coogan. "Ike, I'll never forget you!" That morning even Ike did not seem to smell too bad.

"Get away!" the old man howled. "What the hell you doin' anyway? You some kind of morphodite? Men don't hug each other — leastways not where I come from!"

"I love you!" Charlie grinned, to Ike's further embarrassment, and to the astonishment of some of the miners who were working downstream. "Good-bye, Ike!"

He traveled downriver in style in the California Steam Navigation Company's *San Joaquin* paddlewheeler. At the Pacific Street landing he stepped off the boat and decided San Francisco was not a pretty town. Weathered and shabby houses were built on piles driven into the sand. The air stank of rotting fish and sewage. Pacific Street itself was a muddy lane, lined with "auction palaces," cheap groggeries with names like Bull Run, Cock o' the Walk, and the Rosebud. For five cents a citizen could blow into a "lung-testing machine" operated by Professor Duffy. There were dance halls through the open doors of which came the strains of the fiddle and drum, even this early in the morning. A painted and frizzy-haired harlot in a sleazy shift sauntered from a doorway.

"How about a little nookie, friend? Only a dollar for fifteen minutes!"

"No," Charlie said hastily, tipping his hat. "Thank you, ma'am."

There were peeling posters on the walls:

Here you will find plain talk and beautiful girls!
No back numbers but as sweet and charming
creatures as ever escaped a female seminary!

Another, in screaming red letters, proclaimed:

If you don't want to risk both optics, shut one eye!
Really girly girls! Lovely tresses, lovely lips!
Buxom forms! Seeing is believing! Admission fifty
cents, and a bargain!

Charlie did not know the address of Lorna's Uncle
Matthew except that she had once told him it was in an
area called the Western Addition. But the mission she
had so often talked about, he remembered, was in Little
China. From a strolling policeman he learned that
Little China was on upper Sacramento Street.

In Little China there was poverty and despair. Miserable-
looking women huddled in doorways, dull-eyed babies
in their arms. A sweetish smell hovered in the air.
Charlie recognized it as burning opium; one of his old
clan, the riverboat gamblers, had smoked opium in a
small brass-bowled pipe. Mysterious-looking men in
flat-crowned hats and severe black walked about in
troops; some kind of Chinese police, Charlie figured.
Naked children, bony and undernourished, cried out
with thin wails as Charlie passed, holding out hands
for alms. Ugliness, disease, and vice were rampant, and
over all was the stench of excrement, rotting food,
and laundry steam.

At the corner of Washington Street, just beyond Kearney, he paused, unbelieving. Below was what looked like the pit of hell; a subterranean anthill into which the denizens of Little China descended on rickety ladders. Huddled bodies lay about in the thin autumn sunshine. Beggars crouched along the walls, holding out tin cups. The pit was lined with small makeshift shelters — huts of cardboard, tin, discarded lumber, broken bricks, ancient canvas. Sick and diseased people tottered about, fell, lay senseless in the squalor. Stomach queasy, Charlie turned away. San Francisco, the golden gate, the city of opportunity and fortune!

In response to his queries he found no one who spoke English. Passersby stared at him with almond eyes, shook their heads, hurried on. Walking endlessly, he found himself near the bay again, and spoke to a Jewish tailor sitting cross-legged before his shop.

"Christian Mission to the Chinese, young man?" The tailor's English was heavily accented. "Could be." He cocked his head, needle poised, thinking. "Used to was a place like that in Brooklyn Alley."

"Hewitt? The Reverend Matthew Hewitt?"

"I know many people. *Mein Gott,* so many come to have pants fixed! But no Hewitt."

Charlie hastened back to Little China. In Brooklyn Alley he found no Christian Mission to the Chinese. The lane was short and narrow, occupied almost completely by a series of cribs with upswept eaves from which came the minor tones of some kind of plucked instrument and a woman's high-pitched laughter.

194

Frustrated, Charlie bought a dried fish from a passing vendor and squatted in the shade of an awning. What now?

Making shooing motions with his hands, the owner of the shop emerged gabbling in Chinese.

"Go to hell!" Charlie said. "I'm not hurting your damned place!"

The moon-faced man spoke in singsong English. "You bad for business!"

Throwing away the salty fish, Charlie rose. "Tell me, sir — do you know of a place called the Christian Mission to the Chinese?"

The Chinaman pursed fat lips. "You go away?"

"Yes, if you'll tell me —"

"Mission no more." The Chinaman waved plump hands. "Revvum Hewitt die. Little Pete tear down mission."

"Who is Little Pete?"

"You not know?"

"I don't know."

The shop owner giggled. "You stupid white man!"

"Maybe. But I am looking for Reverend Hewitt's niece. A girl. A pretty girl."

"White girls no pretty!"

"That's beside the point!" Charlie was getting upset. "Her name was — is — Lorna. Lorna Bascomb. She was — is — Reverend Hewitt's niece. Do you know her?"

The man's face was somber. "Revvum Hewitt do good work for poor Chinaman. He good white man."

"Do you know Lorna Bascomb?"

"Missy Bascomb good white woman. Help Chinese."

"Where in God's name can I find her, then? Please!"

"Probary at Palace Hotel. Help poor people again."

"Palace Hotel?"

"Washington Street, by Kearney."

"Thanks!" Charlie rushed off, in his haste pushing aside the small Chinese and drawing muttered curses. At Washington and Kearney he paused, heart beating fast, searching for the Palace Hotel. Palace Hotel? There was no Palace Hotel. Anxiously he buttonholed passersby again, drawing only blank stares.

"Palace Hotel," he repeated for the hundredth time. "Can you tell me — where is the Palace Hotel?"

An old woman tottered by on bound feet, eyes fixed on the ground; she was carrying a dead chicken by the neck. Charlie grabbed her stringy arm. "Please, ma'am — can you tell me where to find the Palace Hotel?"

Her thin lips moved in a grimace. "Palace — Hotel?" The old woman started to laugh, a grim cackling.

"Yes! The Palace Hotel!"

The evil harpy, garbed in rusty funereal black, turned slowly, pointing. "There — Palace Hotel"

Unbelieving, he stared again at the subterranean anthill. Some — some white wag — must have named the place. Down there, in the sickness and squalor and poverty — Lorna Bascomb?

"I — I thank you," he muttered. Still cackling, the crone tottered on, dead chicken swinging at her side. Charlie stood at the edge of the pit of hell. The sun had disappeared in a veil of clouds and it began to rain, a thin veil that compounded the misery below. He heard a distant peal of thunder; a jagged streak of lightning laced the sky.

"I haven't heard from you in a long time," Charlie muttered to the Old Gentleman. "But if you're not too blasted busy picking your nose up there, see what you can do to help Lorna!" Wrapping the new coat tightly about him against the chill rain, he went toward the rickety ladder leading down into the Palace Hotel. "And while you're at it," he added, "give me a hand too! I'm going to get her out of this hole!"

CHAPTER
ELEVEN

After waiting his turn among the human ants who swarmed up and down, he descended the rickety ladder. Curious black eyes followed him as he walked through the sordid passages and alleyways of the Palace Hotel. Giving way before his purposeful stride, the Chinese drew away and murmured among themselves; something that sounded like *lo-fan*.

"Lorna!" he called, at random, "Lorna Bascomb!" A legless beggar on a wheeled platform scuttled about and Charlie blocked his way with a boot. "Lorna?" he asked. "Lorna Bascomb!" When the man only shook his pig-tailed head, Charlie shouted at him. "Do — you — know — a — white woman — named Lorna Bascomb?" The man scowled, wheeled angrily away.

Dull-eyed children with sores on cheeks, bare arms and legs, watched him. A withered old man lay in the dirt, eyes closed, like a wax figure. Dead? Charlie shrank away, then smelled the sweetish bouquet of opium; not dead, only drugged to forget the squalid surroundings. An old lady knelt at the man's side, weeping; he handed her a coin and hurried on.

That was a mistake. Begging with outstretched palms, a crowd of children pursued him. "No!" he shouted. "Go away!" Finally their desperate eyes overcame him. He emptied his pockets of coins and hurried off, leaving the children scrabbling like starved chickens after a handful of corn.

"Lorna! Lorna Bascomb!" Bewildered, he found himself in a dead-end passage fetid with the stink of excrement, spoiled food, sickness — death. A dead cat lay in a pool of water, and a shutter was quickly closed. He shook his head, started to turn back. But a small wiry man in a stained singlet barred the way; he drew a knife from his belt and held out his hand.

"Wallet," he said.

"Eh?"

"You give wallet," the bandit insisted.

"I'll be damned if I will!"

Crouching, knife held low and blade up, the Chinese approached. Charlie had seen that use of a knife before: held low, so as not to be grasped by a victim, and blade up to rip through the belly. Looking frantically about for a weapon, he found none. He backed away until he brushed against the bamboo mats that enclosed a rude dwelling.

"Get away from me!" In desperation he raised his only defense, a boot. He had seen a boot to the groin used to good effect, but what use was it against a knife-wielding Chinaman? His assailant had probably skewered more than a few victims.

"*Ai — eeeee!*" Screaming curses, an old woman in ragged blouse and pantaloons, rag wrapped around her head, hurried into the cul-de-sac. Carrying a wicker basket filled with drooping vegetables, she battered the knife-bearer with it, swinging the basket like a club. Carrots, eggplant, spinach, beets, beans — all flew into the air as she beat the assassin. "*Ai — eeeee!*" She erupted like fireworks, Chinese fireworks, crying out what must have been some powerful Cantonese curses, and waving a tattered umbrella.

Trying to shield his skull from the blows, the Chinaman cowered. Finally he fled, running low and fast, forgetting the knife.

"Aha!" the old lady said, or something like that. A crucifix swung from a chain about her withered neck as she kicked the gleaming knife into a pile of rubbish and knelt to pick up the scattered vegetables.

Charlie hurried to help. "I'm very grateful, ma'am," he said, blowing out a deep and relieved breath. "He'd have spilled my giblets all over this alley if you hadn't come along!"

Vegetables restored, the old lady spoke. "You look Missy Bascomb?"

Wide-eyed, Charlie stared. "Yes! Yes, indeed! Lorna Bascomb! Do you know where she is?"

The old lady crooked a bony finger. "You come along me."

She must have followed him, heard his questioning of the passersby. So he went along with her. Winding through a wilderness of small shops, tents, dwellings too primitive even to be called shanties, they came at last to a dark doorway. Though the rain had stopped and a few scattered rays of sun shone into the depths of the Palace Hotel, the room was almost in darkness, lit only by a flickering candle.

200

"You go in," she urged.

Cautiously Charlie entered, trying to adjust his eyes to the gloom. Was this only another dead end, one assassin displaced by another? Hair prickled the back of his neck; his skin tingled with the expectation of the sting of a knife sliding between his ribs. In the flickering shadows of the candle he at last made out a rude cot. On the cot lay a Chinese woman clad only in a shift; on her stomach was a newborn infant, the cord still not cut. Back to him, another Chinese woman was washing her hands in a basin, drying them on a clean rag.

"Lorna?"

She turned. The woman was not Chinese. She was Lorna Bascomb.

"I'm Lorna Bascomb, sir. What do you want of me?"

Charlie was shocked. It was indeed Lorna Bascomb, a pale and haggard Lorna, deep circles under her eyes, dark hair pulled back in an untidy knot. She was dressed in worn and shabby Chinese garments — loose-fitting blouse, pantaloons, black felt slippers.

"Lorna! It's Charlie! Charlie Callaway! What in God's name has happened to you?"

She knew him then and ran to him, throwing her arms about him. "Charlie! Oh, Charlie! I — I knew you'd come someday!" She began to weep.

He stroked the dark hair. "There, there, now! It will be all right, Lorna! Charlie's here!"

Her body shook with the intensity of her sobbing. "Charlie! It's — it's a miracle! Oh, Charlie! If you only knew how I've hoped — how I dreamed —" She clutched his arm so hard it was painful, but he didn't care. "Charlie, it's you!"

"Yes," he said again. "It's me, my dear. But what — how —"

Cheeks tearstained, she wiped her eyes with the hem of the blouse. "I — I can't explain, now. There's so much to be done." She knelt beside the cot. "This poor woman has had such a hard time!"

The old lady put down her basket and spoke in Chinese. Lorna hesitated, answered in the same language. A short colloquy followed. Finally Lorna nodded, rose. The old lady picked up a pair of scissors.

"Dah Pah Tsin will take care of the rest," she explained. "Charlie, come with me, where we can talk!"

Before a noodle shop they sat on a rotting packing box. Charlie looked warily into his bowl.

"It's really good," Lorna assured him. "And cheap! Don't be afraid!"

While they ate noodles and drank tea from a tin pot — fifteen pennies for the lot — Lorna told her story. At times her voice broke and she could not go on. Charlie waited patiently while curious children surrounded the pair.

"*Lo-fan*, they are saying," Lorna explained. "That means foreigner. No white man ever comes down here. Anyway, when Uncle Matthew died, I tried to take over the mission. But there wasn't any money. He had mortgaged everything to keep the mission going. Aunt Carrie died shortly after that — from pure grief, I think. Then Little Pete evicted us from the mission."

202

"Little Pete, eh?" Charlie remembered the moon-faced Chinaman who had tried to chase him away from his shop. "You not know who is Little Pete? You stupid white man!"

Lorna leaned wearily against him. "Charlie, I can't believe you're here. Any minute now I'm going to wake up and —"

"Little Pete," he repeated. "Tell me about Little Pete."

Lorna shuddered. "He is an evil man, the most evil! Uncle Matthew thought him a reincarnation of Beelzebub! His real name in Fung Jin Toy, and he is the uncrowned emperor of Little China! They call him King of the Tongs. He hated Uncle Matthew and the mission, and when I tried to take it over he said the mission was just causing trouble. What he meant was that the poor people were pledging their allegiance to Jesus Christ instead of to Little Pete, and that made him angry!"

"He is powerful, then?"

"He is head of the Six Companies and he *owns* Little China. He is so powerful that the politicians from downtown come to him when they want something. He is in league with them, you see. I think they get a share of the profits from the gambling and prostitution he is engaged in."

"Gambling, eh?"

She laid down the empty bowl. "Every night one can see the carriages of rich men — aldermen, city officials, bankers, merchants. They come to Little Pete's headquarters at Waverly Place and Washington Street to

— to lie with the beautiful slave girls and play cards at high stakes. I have heard that even the mayor owes Little Pete gambling debts." She suddenly paused, eyes wide. "Charlie, you — you —"

He was puzzled. "I — what?"

She eyed his new clothes, the prosperous look, the gold watchchain across his flowered silk vest. "You are gambling again! Oh, Charlie!"

"I am not!" he protested. "Lorna, I have given up gambling! I am a changed man! You do not know what I have gone through to make myself worthy of you!" In spite of the stares of coolies passing with baskets of laundry and of other curious passersby, of the butcher with his poor stock of fly-covered meat, he kissed her. "Now, my dear, I am going to take you away from all this! You see, I was in the gold mines near Sacramento, and my partner and I came on a store of nuggets in the river. My share was almost a thousand dollars! We can get married, Lorna, and rent a little house! We can —"

"No!"

He stared at her. "What?"

"I cannot!"

"But —"

"You don't want me, Charlie! I'm not the Lorna Bascomb you once knew! Just look at me!"

"I don't care! Lorna, I love you, and only you! If you only knew how I've dreamed of you, dreamed of this day, wanted you. Lorna, I *need* you!"

"Charlie, these poor people need me more. Since the mission has gone there is no one to help them — no one to give them courage to feed them when they are

204

hungry, to nurse them when they are ill. I would be false to Uncle Matthew if I ran away."

"But Lorna —"

"No!" Her chin was high, firm. He remembered that look when she told him she could never marry him because of the gambling. "There is no use arguing, Charlie."

Crushed, he put down the half-eaten noodles.

"I am sorry, truly sorry." She put a comforting hand on his. "Charlie, believe me — someday, good will prevail! Someday the Lord will favor the poor Chinese with his generosity, his love, his compassion. Someday I shall establish another Christian Mission to the Chinese here to carry on Uncle Matthew's work. Someday I will build a bigger and better mission, one with a small hospital, storehouses for food, an assembly hall where God's word can be brought to these poor people. God will help me, Charlie — I am sure of that! In the meantime I must go on doing what I can. Do you understand?"

Charlie was brokenhearted. "I guess so, Lorna," he murmured.

Dah Pah Tsin emerged from an alleyway and beckoned to Lorna. "Trouble," she said. "Baby sick!"

"I must go." Lorna rose. "Charlie?"

Still dazed, he murmured, "Yes, Lorna?"

"You will be here, for a while? I mean — in San Francisco?"

He nodded. "I will take a room somewhere. Perhaps I can help you in some way." Remembering Reverend

Purdy on O'Fallon Street in St. Louis, he added, "I know the mission business. I once —"

But she was gone, blowing him a kiss. For a long time he sat on the splintered packing box, oblivious to the rush of squalid life about him. Slowly he began to regain a portion of his previous buoyancy. A small boy dared to approach him. Dirty fingers in mouth, he stared at Charlie. "Penny?"

Charlie was deep in thought. "God will help me," Lorna had said. "I am sure of that!"

Slowly he got to his feet. "Penny?"

The child nodded in delight. Charlie searched in his pockets; no pennies. Taking out his wallet, he gave the urchin a bill. "God will help me!"

Shrieking with joy, the little boy ran off, holding high the bank note. Charlie climbed the ladder again. Pausing at the top, he looked down into the scurrying anthill. Maybe, he thought, God could use a little help, too.

Daily, attired in black broadcloth frock coat and vest to match, crowned by a wide-brimmed planter's felt hat and smoking an expensive cigar, Colonel Charles Chaney of Chattanooga, Tennessee, drove through the crowded streets of Chinatown in a rented barouche, fondling the massive gold chain draped across his chest. Chaney was a handsome man of considerable height, with a sweeping white mustache and delicately trimmed pointed beard. A massive gold ring sparkled on his finger. From time to time he negligently tossed coins to the band of urchins that followed the carriage, smiling

206

benevolently. He did not long escape public notice. A reporter from the *San Francisco Call*, writing an article on the vicious and immoral habits of the Chinese, interviewed him.

"Where are you from, sir?"

For a moment Colonel Chaney puffed on his cigar. After a pause, he said, "From many parts, sir, in my business. But I call the lovely old town of Chattanooga, Tennessee, my ancestral home. President Andrew Johnson, you know, is from Tennessee. Andrew and I were good friends."

The reporter's face lit up and he-scribbled furiously. "What line of business are you in, colonel?"

Chaney sighed, grimaced as though in pain. "I entreat you, sir, do not use my military title! I was terribly wounded in the battle of Gettysburg when I was with A. P. Hill's Third Corps. The sound of a military title brings back disturbing memories."

"I'm sorry, sir."

"That's all right." The colonel, a sober and reflective man, paused again. "I am here on business. As you know, the war is over. The slaves who formerly worked our great plantations in the South have been freed. No man can quarrel with that; it was a just action on the part of our martyred President. I have often wept to see my overseers whip the poor devils. But now we must find other labor to till our fields, plant the seeds, harvest the cotton, sing the touching old songs our darkies once entertained us with as we sat on the veranda of an evening sipping juleps."

"You don't sound Southern," the reporter observed.

Hastily Colonel Chaney explained. "I was brought up in an exclusive school in Philadelphia and lived there for several years. It was not until the affair at Fort Sumter that I returned home and joined up."

"I see."

"So, young man, I have decided to visit California to see if it is practicable to buy up several thousand Chinese to be transported to the South as field hands."

The reporter almost dropped his notebook. "You mean —"

"I am," the colonel said, "a man accustomed to great enterprises. Perhaps, some might say, a bit of a gambler. But if my plan succeeds —"

"Jesus Christ!" the reporter marveled. "Just think of it! San Francisco has been trying to get rid of the Chinese for years!"

The colonel nodded. "Just so." He waved to the driver of his barouche. "Now, sir, I take my leave! I have further investigations to carry on."

The *Call* made a headline story of the event. San Francisco was excited. "The Chinese," the *Call* reported, "have manners and habits that are repugnant to decent men and women of the white race. Of different language, blood, religion, and character, they are only a little superior to the Negro. Still, they would make satisfactory field hands for Colonel Chaney's extensive cotton plantations in the South. It is to be hoped that this cultured Southern gentleman will succeed in his great enterprise, solving his own problems as well as a pressing one for our great city. The *Call* entreats all citizens to assist the colonel (a modest man who does not like to be called by his military title) in every way possible."

The colonel spent much of his time in the gambling halls, dropping a considerable amount of money at faro in the Pacific Club on Commercial Street and the Aguila de Oro on Montgomery. He only shrugged; "Easy come, easy go!" Billy Briggs, who ran the Arcade near Portsmouth Square, invited the colonel into his office. After pouring him two fingers of imported Scotch whiskey, he said, "Colonel, maybe you'd be interested in the game at Little Pete's."

The colonel fondled the gold and ivory head of his walking stick. "Little Pete?"

"Real name's Fung Jin Toy. He's the boss in Little China. You'd have to deal with Little Pete anyway to get the slaves — I mean the workers — you want. A high-stakes draw poker game goes on there. The mayor and the aldermen and all the high muckety-mucks of the city play. For your business it might be a good idea to get to know them."

The colonel pursed his lips. "Thank you, sir. I'll think about it."

At night, after turning in the rented carriage, Charlie slipped covertly into the shabby rented room in the upper part of Sacramento Street. Did anyone see him? Inside, he locked the door and turned up the lamp. Dah Pah Tsin and the other Chinese awaited him. Beside the old woman sat the frail Loi San, peeling carrots. The others crowded round, expectant.

"It's working!" he exulted. "They've taken the bait!"

Loi San helped him off with his coat while Lem Duck, the one-time actor at the Imperial Court, gently peeled off the mustaches and beard. When Charlie had shaken the flour out of his hair, Dah Pah Tsin handed him a cup of tea from a brass pot simmering over a brazier.

"Take — bait?" Dah Pah Tsin asked, puzzled.

"Means they'll soon ask me to join the big game at Little Pete's!" Charlie hurried over to the lamp-lit alcove where the old dollmaker was working. "How is it coming?"

The little man in the ragged blue jumper held up a polished ivory rod, showing how it fit into a socket of jade.

"Good!" Charlie smiled, nodded. "Very good. You — are — the — best!" To Dah Pah Tsing he asked, "Lorna doesn't suspect?"

"She not know nothing! We" — she waved at the other Chinese — "very clever, all! Not worry, Misser Charlie!"

He sighed with relief. "This masquerade is the hardest work I've ever done. But there's a good chance it will pay off!"

Loi San gently touched his sweaty brow with her kerchief. He slumped on the sagging cot, refusing the bowl of noodles. "I'm too tired to eat, child. Maybe after I snooze a little —"

He was asleep before he knew it.

The invitation was not long in coming. Since his stake from the nuggets was disappearing at an alarming rate, what with carriage hire, gambling at the casinos, and expensive clothing, he took instead to walking about Little China, swinging the walking stick and smoking less expensive cigars; there needed to be a considerable amount left when the fateful time arrived. On a blistering hot day he was strolling Waverly Place near Little Pete's garish headquarters when someone tapped him on the shoulder. With the caution of long experience as a fugitive, he turned quickly. "Eh? Who is it?"

A platoon of stolid-faced *boo how doy* in black coats and flat-brimmed hats surrounded him. The leader, a scar-faced man, burly for a Chinese, tipped the flat hat. "You come along me, please, sir?"

"What for?"

"Master say bring you. He want to talk, chop-chop."

"Oh? And who, I pray, is this master of yours?"

"Fung Jin Toy. Little Pete. He say, bring you."

"Very well, then."

Four before and four behind, with scouts on the flanks, they accompanied him into the red and yellow building with the sharply upswept eaves adorned with toothy dragons. Inside it was dim, odorous with incense and the sweetish scent of opium. From behind a latticework screen came muffled giggles. Slave girls, he thought. Poor wretches!

In formation the hatchet men led him up carpeted stairways, down intricate passageways, through a bewildering thicket of narrow aisles and balconies high above the teeming street. Pausing at each, the leader muttered some kind of password. Charlie began to sweat with the effort of climbing stairs. He also had a feeling of near-panic as he was taken deeper into the rabbit warren. Still, he had entered the game and would have to play out his hand. Managing a poker face, he followed the bobbing dark backs before him, listening to the dull boom of a gong somewhere.

At last, high above the street, the procession paused before a massive oaken door carved with writhing dragons and grotesque human faces. The leader knocked, spoke in Cantonese. There was a pause; then the door swung open on well-oiled hinges. Another saffron face appeared, beckoned. They entered an anteroom.

"Sir, you wait here," the leader said.

Trying to look indifferent, Charlie shrugged. "Very well. But tell your master I have important business to transact this afternoon with a group of bankers on Lombard Street!"

After a while the leader returned. "You go in now!" Charlie sauntered in, swinging the walking stick.

Little Pete sat at a huge desk at the far end of the room, a desk so large that he only peered over the edge, plump face spangled with sweat.

"You Colonel Chaney — yes?"

Charlie nodded. "I am he, sir."

Little Pete waved a bejeweled hand. "You sit down there, in chair, please!"

Charlie sat, crossed his legs. "What do you want of me, sir?"

Little Pete beamed. "You want Chinamen plant cotton, hoe weeds, work on plantation like slaves?"

Charlie cleared his throat, chose his words carefully. "So you have heard about my idea?"

"Everybody hear! You big man!"

Charlie shook a hand in deprecation. "Only a Southern planter, sir, trying to restore the South to its rightful economic place among the other states which drubbed us so badly in the unfortunate war!"

"You like Chinese girl?"

Charlie was taken aback. "Un — not right now, thank you."

"I find you plenty field hands. How many you need?"

"You understand, Mr. Pete —"

"You call me just Pete — yes?"

"You understand that this is all very tentative. There would have to be negotiations with the federal authorities, with the governor of Tennessee, with the citizens of our great state. I am not at all sure I will be successful. But as a public-spirited man I am trying to do what I can to restore the ravaged economy of my beloved South. Until I have made further investigations I cannot put a precise figure on our needs. And — as I say — the whole plan may come to naught. Who knows?"

Little Pete was disappointed. "Well, I help all I can, colonel. When you need Chinamen, you come me — yes? I furnish a hundred, a thousand!" He grinned evilly. "Got plenty Chinamen here in Little China. Too damn many! They give trouble! I like get rid of Chinamen, especial troublemaker!"

"I will remember," Charlie promised. Waiting for something more, he hesitated before rising. At last it came.

Squat and barrel-shaped in the embroidered robe, rich with brocade and intricate needlework, Little Pete rose.

"You gamble — yes?"

Charlie laughed negligently. "Oh, I enjoy a bout with the pasteboards!"

"Paste — boards?"

"That's what we call them in Chattanooga. Just means — cards. Poker, you know. Stud, draw, whatever."

"You come play here." Little Pete pointed to a large round table covered with green felt standing in an alcove. "You welcome any time, colonel! My good friends — mayor and aldermen, police inspector, officers from Presidio — we play every week."

Charlie rubbed his chin, appearing to think. When Little Pete started to say something, he broke in quickly. "Why, that's mighty white of you, sir!" He bit his lip; "white of you" was a mistake with Little Pete's lemon-colored skin. Little Pete did not notice. He took Charlie's hand in his own sweaty clutch and waddled with him to the door.

"You come any time," he invited. "You welcome! Anything you want — Chinese girl, opium, liquor! Next Thursday we play."

Charlie bowed. "Thank you, sir."

Little Pete called after him. "Remember — got lots Chinaman! Whenever you ready!"

Again the *boo how doy* escorted him down the stairs, through the narrow passageways, balconies, and iron-hinged doors. Coming out on Waverly Place, the leader raised his hat politely.

"Thank you, sir."

"Thank *you!*" Charlie said.

214

Glad to be out of the place, elated with success, he hurried toward the room on Sacramento Street, taking many false turns and backtracking to avoid anyone who might be following. At the doorway of the rented room he turned, searching the street. A noodle-vendor passed, clanging a small bell. A shopkeeper dozed in his doorway in the heat. A small girl played with a ragged doll. In the middle of the street an oily trickle of sewage stitched its way toward the bay. It looked safe. To make sure, he walked quickly around the block, returned. The noodle-vendor was gone; he could now hear only the faint clang of the bell. The merchant had vanished inside and closed his shutters. The little girl stared at him, went on playing with the doll. The sewage still trickled on. So far, so good!

Inside, his friends awaited him in the airless gloom. Old Dah Pah Tsin was concerned.

"We worry you," she said. "You gone so long."

The false beard and mustache came easily from his sweating face. "I've done it!" he cried.

They looked at him. "Do — what?"

"Little Pete has invited me to play poker with the high brass this coming Thursday! The aldermen, police inspector, high-rankers from the Presidio! Now —" He turned toward the fetid alcove where Loo Chee, the dollmaker, was fitting together an assembly of delicately fashioned parts. "When will you finish it?"

The old man held up the complicated assembly he had put together from Charlie Callaway's sketches. "Pretty soon."

"That's not soon enough," Charlie protested. "It's got to be done by *Thursday!* That's when the big game is!"

"Thursday?" Loo Chee shook his pig-tailed head. "No can do!"

"But you've got to! This business is very wearing on the nerves, and I've got to strike while the iron is hot!" In despair Charlie turned to Dah Pah Tsin. "You explain it to him, please, ma'am!"

"I tell him," she said. Bursting into a torrent of Cantonese, she waved her hands and pulled the old man about by the neck of his tattered blouse. At last, intimidated, Loo Chee nodded.

"All right! I do!"

Charlie seized Dah Pah Tsin and Loi San and danced about the room in an awkward jig.

"Thursday!" he cried. "Lucky Thursday! It's going to be the best Thursday that ever was!"

CHAPTER
TWELVE

With great pride Loo Chee held up the final product of his labors — a network of ivory rods, telescoping tubes, sliding joints, silken straps, and powerful elastic bands. The holdout was Charlie Callaway's design, but with a definite Oriental flavor. The delicate assembly was designed to reach from a man's forearm to his shoulders and down to his knees. The gambler had only to spread his knees slightly and the "sneak" moved from the coat sleeve to deposit a needed card into his hand.

"Beautiful!" Charlie cried. "Loo Chee, you are a genius!"

Loo Chee did not know what a genius was, but it was obvious Charlie was praising him. Tucking gnarled hands into his sleeves, he bowed.

Charlie was never without a deck of cards in his pocket. Selecting the ace of spades, he tucked it into the jaws of the sneak.

"Now let me try it on!" With Dah Pah Tsin and Loi San assisting, he got into the harness and put on his coat. Sitting at the table, he spread his knees. Like a well-oiled machine the sneak slipped an ace into his hand.

"My God!" he said reverently. "With this thing a man could sit at a table and win all of San Francisco —

the ships, the wharves, Telegraph Hill, the big houses
— everything!" Still, he reminded himself to be cautious,
remembering Nathan Goodbody's words when discussing
the simple but not too effective breastplate holdout
Nathan had once used on the boats. "Holding out one
card will beat any square game in the world. Holding
out two cards is very strong. Never hold out more than
three. One is really enough because you are playing six
cards against every one else's five, and the odds are
bound to tell. It looks better if you play the machine on
someone else's deal, though. In a big game, never use
the machine more than three or four times a night. But
remember — the machine is only part of the game! If
you're going to use it, practice, practice, practice! The
machine is only as good as the man using it. And if
you're caught, there's no way out! With all that machinery
under your coat, you're a dead duck!"

"Ma'am," he said to Dah Pah Tsin, "you can't imagine
how magical this machine is! You know magic?"

"Know Chinese magic!"

"This is Charlie Callaway magic, ma'am! With this
marvelous machine I'm going to get Lorna her mission
back, along with maybe the hospital she wanted, and
money to buy food for all the poor and sick people in
the Palace Hotel! Then — you know what?"

"Know what?" the old woman muttered, frying fish
in a skillet.

"I'm going to marry Lorna! I'm going to marry her
and we'll live in a big house on a hill and have lots of
children and I'm never going to gamble again!"

"Maybe!"

218

"Maybe what? I tell you — it's going to work! Nathan Goodbody himself said I was the best operator he'd ever seen! And Lorna and I have got you and Loo Chee and Loi San and Lem Duck to thank for our happiness!" Excited, he wolfed down the food, the rice and pork Dah Pah Tsin put on his plate. "You're sure Lorna doesn't suspect anything?"

"She no — sus — sus —"

"Good. And Colonel Chaney?"

"No one sus — sus —"

"Excellent!" Buoyant, he took out his sweet potato; he hadn't played it for a long time. Dah Pah Tsin, however, looked doubtful.

"What's the matter?" he asked. "Don't you like music?"

"Like Chinese music! Not *that!*"

Charlie grinned. "Come Thursday, I'll hire a Chinese band to sit at your window and play all day while you lie on a silken couch and eat sweetmeats!"

"Maybe!"

After endless practice sessions with the holdout, Thursday came. With the thrill he always felt before a big game, Charlie took a carriage to Little Pete's headquarters at Washington Street and Waverly Place. At the door, paying the hack driver liberally, he shot his cuffs, spread his knees, feeling the holdout noiselessly slide and fold and articulate; it lay on him like a feather. Steamboat playing cards were common. He had loaded the claw with the Steamboat ace of spades; of course, if they were using a different deck, he would have to deal himself an extra card to load the sneak.

Lighting a Havana, he strolled to Little Pete's headquarters. To play the role of Colonel Charles Chaney of Chattanooga had been more expensive than he had planned. Out of almost a thousand dollars he had realized from his share of the American River nuggets, he had remaining only a little over seven hundred. He would, of course, lose a few pots to allay suspicion, but would play the rest carefully to accomplish his ends. There would be no deal unless a great amount were at stake.

One of the *boo how doy* opened the door, bowing low; the colonel was expected. Again he followed the Chinaman up the stairways, across the balconies, through the endless passageways and corridors and teakwood doors. Finally, from the other end of the long hall he heard bantering voices, smelled tobacco smoke, sniffed the bouquet of Kentucky whiskey.

"Misser Colonel Chaney," the hatchet man announced, opening the inner door. "He come!"

Little Pete, bowing and scraping, came himself to the door, rubbing fat hands. "Ah — Colonel Chaney! So glad you come!" He introduced Charlie to the rest of the players. "Meet Captain Post — own big fleet barge and boat! Meet Neville, editor of *Call* — name Henry Neville. You meet bank man George Roland!" Little Pete giggled. "He got lots money!"

Mr. Roland looked pained.

"Gents, this Colonel Chaney you hear so much about! Colonel, meet Deputy Mayor Backus, Luther

220

Backus! Funny name, eh? Luther — Backside!" Little Pete giggled again.

Someone handed him a drink but Charlie declined. He must keep his wits about him. "After the war," he demurred, "I took the pledge, gentlemen! I once saw a whole warehouse of Georgia corn whiskey burned by that rascal Cump Sherman. The sight so saddened me that I have not been able to touch a drop of spirits since!"

Charlie quickly chose a chair against the wall so no one could get behind him. They sat at the big green-felt-covered table, puffing cigars, sipping whiskey, telling jokes. Deputy Mayor Backus, a gaunt and cadaverous man with a fringe of chin whiskers, turned to Charlie. "Did you hear the one, colonel, about the —"

There was a chorus of good-humored raillery. "Luther, if you tell that one about the parson's daughter again, we're going to blackball you!"

Charlie joined in the laughter. "Perhaps," he said, "if you gentlemen will permit me —"

"Go ahead, colonel! Go ahead!"

"I'll give you a little Tennessee humor, then." He told them the old one about the newcomer to a small town who wanted to join an exclusive man's club. They hung on Charlie's every word. Finally Charlie came to the snapper. "I thought you told me to wrestle a Tennessee girl and make love to a bear!"

They howled with delight, slapped him on the back, vowed he was a good fellow, and stated they looked forward to more of his company.

Little Pete did not understand the joke. Rapping on the table with the handle of his silken fan, he grumbled, "Now we play cards, yes? I deal first. Five-card draw!" He broke the seal on a new deck of Steamboat cards — Charlie had rarely seen cards of any other manufacture — and dealt them out, counting in Cantonese. Captain Post, a grizzled sea dog, was annoyed.

"Talk English, Pete! Nobody don't understand that heathen gabble!"

Little Pete grinned, bowed sitting down. "I forget."

Charlie picked up his cards. A pair of nines, seven of spades, five of hearts, trey of clubs; not much, but it could be improved. He stayed for a dollar ante, and drew three cards to the pair of nines. Fanning out the cards, he stared at a third nine. It was tempting, but too early in the game to start winning. When Deputy Mayor Backus bet two dollars, he threw down his cards. "Didn't hit," he explained, and lit a fresh Havana.

The game went on, Charlie carefully avoiding winning a pot but always coming close. "Dame Fortune is geographically sensitive," he complained. "In Tennessee my luck runs much better. Must be something in the salt air climate out here that obfuscates my cards!"

Mentally he was making notes. Captain Post was a fair player, but inclined to recklessness. Woolly-eyebrowed Editor Neville was cautious, but sound; he appeared to be laying back for a big pot. Sour-looking Banker Roland hated to risk his stake; that was to be expected from a banker. Deputy Mayor Backus was a talker. Charlie noted he was inclined to cover his actions with a fog of small talk; Backus was to be watched. And Little Pete, smoking opium in a long-stemmed brass-bowled pipe, was clever. With interest Charlie watched Pete's deal. Was he up against another card manipulator? But no; the King of the Tongs was square — so far — but a wily opponent. Charlie stole a glance at the clock on the wall above an embroidered hanging full of dragons. Only eight-thirty P.M.; still plenty of time to make his move.

He took a small pot with a legitimate pair of queens. With an oath Captain Post threw down a pair of jacks. "Looks like your luck's turning, colonel," Editor Neville remarked.

"Too early to tell," Charlie shrugged.

Without thinking he crossed his legs; the sneak, loaded with the ace of spades, moved into his palm. Fortunately his left hand was below the table and no one noticed but a dew of sweat spangled his forehead. A close call — he swallowed hard to rid his throat of the lump. "And if you're caught, there's no way out! With all that machinery under your coat, you're a dead duck!" Nathan had said. He would have to be more careful with his knees.

The room was warm and humid, fetid with the stink of opium and cigar smoke. Through the open window came the noises of Little China — cries of street vendors, the banging of a drum, a woman's hysterical laugh, the wail of a beggar. In the west a single star hung like a lantern in the sky. Deputy Mayor Backus took off his coat, ran a finger around a wilted paper collar. "Damn it, deal the cards, Henry!"

223

Servants brought tea, small cakes. Captain Post groaned. "Ain't you got any cold beer, Pete?"

Little Pete shrugged. "You drink tea! Good for you!" Tempers were rising; Editor Neville muttered an obscenity.

Charlie won another pot with three deuces. "Small but mighty," he observed, raking in the pot. It was nine-fifteen P.M., and so far he had managed to preserve his stake for the big hand.

To test the holdout he matched an ace of hearts he drew with the ace of spades from the sneak, winning another small pot. "The machine is only as good as the man using it." Well, an honors graduate of the riverboats, taught by Nathan Goodbody himself, was pretty good! Even Nathan had often admired Charlie's skill at dealing seconds — keeping the top card in position until he needed it and dealing out the cards beneath. In addition, Charlie had this night sandpapered his fingertips until they almost bled. Now they tingled, sensitive and responsive, doing his bidding. Picking up the cards for his deal, he calmly sequestered an extra ace, then tossed the rest of his hand into the discards, quickly. In a lull while Captain Post sent out for a bucket of beer, he tucked the ace of hearts in the sneak.

"Well," sighed Editor Neville, "I'm from these parts, colonel, but Lady Luck don't seem to know *me* tonight!" He glanced at the clock. "If the cards don't get better I'm going back to the office. Got a newspaper to get out!"

"You stay!" Little Pete snarled, drawing two cards. "We need you money!"

224

So far Little Pete was the big winner. Charlie, observing him with a calculating eye, assessed Pete's game. Never stay on a pair lower than jacks; draw two cards to the openers to give the impression of a kicker; bluff seldom but push a low hand to the limit when the stakes were high.

Pete smiled at him. "Cards, colonel?" Charlie took three, winning the pot with three treys. Pete looked sour, threw down his cards in disgust. "You got lucky!"

"Oh, it goes around the table," Charlie shrugged.

"Well, I hope she stops here soon!" the deputy mayor grumbled. "I've lost nigh on to a hundred dollars so far!" He had. Little Pete had won most of it, and Charlie the rest; by now he had a pair of aces in the sneak.

Slowly the stakes rose, along with the oppressive summer heat. Little Pete, sweat dripping from the folds of his lemon face, asked, "Why you no take off coat, colonel? Hot in here!"

Charlie stiffened. Making his voice casual, he said, "We Southerners are used to the heat, sir! Besides, in my state it is considered a breach of etiquette for a gentleman to remove his coat when he is a guest in another man's house!"

With a pair of aces put away in the sneak, Charlie played a hand straight, drawing a queen to another queen. The other players, dispirited, dropped out, fanning themselves and helping themselves to the captain's bucket of beer. "Don't know when I've seen it so hot!" Banker Roland complained, picking up Little Pete's painted fan. "Not a breath of air!"

Pete, annoyed, jerked away the fan. "Raise you ten dollar!" he growled to Charlie.

Charlie peered at Pete through narrowed lids. He's bluffing! Already there was over a hundred dollars in bank notes and gold coins on the table. Still, he's not ready for the kill yet. And he's suspicious, Charlie thought. Reluctantly he threw down his hand. "You've got me, Pete. I fold!"

Grinning, Little Pete raked in the pot. "Beat you, colonel!" he crowed.

The street noises grew in volume. The time was ten-thirty. Don't the Chinese ever go to bed? From somewhere below came the deep shuddering clang of a gong and a burst of firecrackers as a procession made its way through the bustle and confusion. After Little Pete's remark about removing his coat, Charlie was getting a mite nervous. Worried, he fondled his beard and burnsides; were they beginning to come loose in the heat? Taking out his wallet, careful to keep his knees together, Charlie drew out two hundred dollars. "This is getting to be an expensive game," he complained.

He let Pete win another pot. Banker Roland took a pot. Pete swept winnings into a wicker basket at his side; the basket was almost full. Now, thought Charlie, Now!

"Your deal," Pete said.

Sweating, Charlie picked up the cards, riffled them awkwardly. "Touch of rheumatism in the fingers," he apologized. Many of the players had lost interest in the game. Charlie had counted on that, offering the deck to Deputy Mayor Backus for a cut. Backus shook his head wearily. "I trust you, colonel." Charlie had left the ace of clubs on top of the deck and dealt seconds masterfully, giving himself the precious third ace — the ace of clubs.

"Open," Little Pete said, throwing ten dollars into the pot. Two players dropped out.

"Call," Charlie said, matching the bet.

Banker Roland drew two cards and looked satisfied. Little Pete drew two. Charlie took two — the seven of hearts and the ace of diamonds. Four aces! His heart tried to explode in his bosom. Calm! he told himself. Calm is the thing, Charlie! His nervousness was compounded when Banker Roland threw down his hand with a sigh.

"It's been a coon's age since I saw an ace!"

"Me, too!" The deputy mayor also threw in his hand. "Maybe," he joked, "we ought to count the cards!" Or was it a joke?

Charlie's hand shook; those *boo how doy*, it was reputed, chopped up their victims with cleavers and put the meat into soups and stews. Nevertheless, in spite of his near-panic, he managed to slip two of the incriminating aces back into the pack and lose the hand to Little Pete. His own sensitive fingers knew that a pack with four cards missing felt light, but he was grateful that no one else in the game had that faculty. He was grateful also that he was sitting against the wall, where no one could observe his manipulations. Still — he had heard that Little Pete's headquarters was sprinkled with sliding panels and false mirrors from behind which the King of the Tongs could spy on malefactors. Pretending to yawn and stretch, he managed a quick glance at the wall behind him. No evidence there, but the Chinese were clever.

"What you look at, colonel?" Little Pete demanded, small button eyes narrowed over his fanned-out cards.

"Nothing, sir! It's just that I had a small crick in my neck, and was trying to relieve it."

It neared midnight. The clamor from below had subsided to some extent but the heat was still oppressive. The deputy mayor's broadcloth shirt was sodden, Banker Roland's mustache dripped small beads of sweat, Captain Post mopped his face with a crumpled handkerchief, Editor Neville fanned himself with Little Pete's brocaded fan. Pete was too intent on the game to notice.

"Sixty dollars," he announced, pushing three double-eagles into the center of the table.

"Too rich for me," Neville decided. The others agreed, threw in their hands. "Getting late, anyway!"

"Call," Charlie said.

They drew cards — Little Pete two, Charlie three. The way Pete was staring at him made if difficult to get at the hidden aces; still, Charlie ended up with a pair of kings and one of the aces which had been returned. Little Pete pushed forward five more double-eagles.

"One hundred dollars."

The others were quiet except for Backus, who sucked in his breath sharply. "Glad I'm out of this game!" he muttered. Push a low hand to the limit when the stakes were high; Charlie remembered his assessment of Little Pete's poker tactics.

"Raise you a hundred," he said.

Pete grimaced. Without hesitation he pushed another stack of coins and a few bank notes across the table. "Raise *you* two hundred, colonel!" The yellow face was greasy with sweat, and his eyes were slits in the fleshy countenance.

"See here!" Captain Post objected. "This was a friendly little game, and now —"

"Call," Charlie said, pushing almost all his remaining funds to the center of the green felt cover. If I lose this, he thought, it's over! Everything for Lorna — it will amount to nothing!

"Well," Neville said impatiently. "Lay down your hands, you two!"

Little Pete shrugged, laid down a pair of kings and three small cards. Swallowing hard, Charlie showed his pair of kings with the ace kicker. "Guess I won," he muttered, trying to keep his voice steady.

Pete's face hardened; he gritted his teeth. When Roland drew out a gold watch and announced that it was after midnight, Pete grabbed the cards. "Not too late! We play one more hand, eh?"

There were protests, but the others finally agreed. "One more hand, then. And that's all, Pete! The game is getting ugly!"

"This seat unlucky!" Pete decided. Standing, he smoothed the long embroidered gown, pulling it away from his rump. "Colonel, you and me — we change seats, eh?"

He is suspicious, Charlie thought. Under his own fashionable coat he was soaked in sweat, not entirely from the heat. "Well — all right." He could hardly refuse his host and keep his reputation as a Southern gentleman. But how in Tophet could he ring in the aces he had in the sneak, sitting as he was in the middle of the room?

It was his deal. The tension in the room was like an India-rubber band stretched to its limit. The other players shifted nervously, stared at their cards, licked lips. Captain Post pulled at his beard; the deputy mayor sucked his teeth.

"Open for a hundred dollars!" Pete announced.

"Christ, Pete —" Neville said, throwing down his cards.

"Me, too." One by one the rest dropped their cards, leaving only Pete and Charlie Callaway.

"Call," Charlie nodded, shoving in a hundred dollars. To the Old Gentleman he murmured, "This is all for Lorna, you know! Damn it — give me some help before I end up as a meat pie in one of those little shops in Portsmouth Square!"

After anteing he still had almost a thousand dollars including his original stake. But with Little Pete so blood-hungry it might take more than that. And if he lost — ! Swallowing a huge lump in his throat, Charlie looked at his cards. Two sevens, a six, a three, and a deuce! Folding his cards, he looked imploringly skyward. Little Pete was amused. "You look for bird up there?" he grinned. "Great bird of fortune, maybe, colonel?"

"It is just my habit when I am thinking."

"Thinking no do good! You have cards or not! Think not pay off! How many cards you want?"

Charlie took three to the pair of sevens. Pete took his usual two. How can I get to those aces in the sneak? Everyone was watching him and Pete with a sort of fascinated dread. I've got to play it straight, he decided. Keep both hands above the table! If this isn't irony! I'm maybe the best cardsharp in the nation, and I've got to risk my damned neck playing the big hand straight! Shakily he fanned out his cards, then closed them quickly. Was that a third seven?

"Bet five hundred!" Little Pete pushed forward a stack of bills.

Cautiously, heart thumping against the restraining straps of the useless holdout, Charlie inspected his hand again. Three sevens! He gulped.

"Well?" Pete's voice was impatient.

"Raise you five hundred!"

Pete's eyes glinted in the yellow folds. "You hit, colonel?" His wicker basket was almost empty.

"Perhaps!"

Pete clapped his hands. A *boo how doy* opened the door, shuffled forward on black felt slippers. In a moment he returned with a black-lacquered chest. Pete opened it with a small brass key and took out packets of bills. Charlie's heart sank. Still — push a low hand to the limit when the stakes are high. That was Pete's game.

Pete laid down ten one-hundred-dollar bills. "Raise *you* five hundred, colonel!"

Charlie could call with the funds he had left but the stakes were not high enough to accomplish what he wanted. He pushed forward five hundred, leaving only a few dollars before him.

"You call, then?" Pete asked.

"No, sir. Not yet!" Charlie took a pencil from his pocket. "May I have a piece of paper?"

Pete scowled. "Why you want paper?"

"I am going to write you a mortgage on a portion of my Tennessee lands, sir. The section is worth — oh, a conservative estimate would put it at five thousand dollars."

Pete started to object but Banker Roland interrupted. "Pete, you started this cutthroat game! I'll back the colonel's note! I am sure he is an honest man. I have dealt with Southerners before, and find them men of honor!"

"Thank you, Mr. Roland." Charlie scribbled, hoping his shakes were not too apparent, and threw the paper into the pool of light under the lamp. Pete's eyes widened; the yellow skin took on a greenish cast.

"All?"

Nodding, Charlie put away the pencil. "All of it! Five thousand dollars, guaranteed by the bank." Lord help me, he thought, but I can do no other! Who said that before? He didn't know but was sure that no one ever expressed it as fervently as he did.

Shaking his head, Pete took out five thousand dollars in bills from the lacquered chest. Now his fat hand trembled. From somewhere came again the melancholy boom of a gong and he started, wiped his forehead. "I — I call," he muttered.

This is it! This is the end of life, or a new beginning! Charlie took a deep breath, laid down his cards. "Three sevens."

Pete stared at the sevens. Then, with a Cantonese imprecation, he tossed his own hand into the air. "Game finish!" he shouted.

Dazed, Charlie raked in the pot. He had won almost six thousand dollars; with his original stake, he now had over seven thousand, along with the worthless note. Carefully he tore the paper into shreds.

"By God, sir, you're a cool one!" the deputy mayor marveled. Captain Post rumbled a laugh. "Is that the way they play poker in Tennessee, colonel? If it is, I'll never go near the place!" Editor Neville said, "I wish there was some way I could write this up for the *Call*! It beats the theater all hollow for drama!"

Charlie saw the malice in Little Pete's eyes. He is getting ready to denounce me, call one of those ugly *boo how doy* to shake me down! Quickly, putting the long-thought-out plan into effect, he spoke.

"I thank you, gentlemen, for letting me play in your most interesting game."

"Colonel —" Little Pete hissed. Charlie talked him down.

"As you know, I came out from my native state with the intention of importing Chinese into Tennessee to work my plantations, now that the black slaves have been freed and do not care any longer to hoe cotton."

"Colonel, you —"

"I am sorry to announce that telegraphic advices from the governor of Tennessee indicate that the public

233

there is opposed to the importation of Chinese labor. It is doubtful, further, that Chinese would flourish on a ration of hominy grits and red-eye gravy. Therefore, I must reluctantly abandon my great enterprise."

"Oh, no!" the deputy mayor protested. "We were hoping —"

"Nevertheless, I am indebted to you all and to the city for receiving my idea so courteously! I must say — I have been very impressed by San Francisco and its citizens. Therefore, before I leave I desire to make a gift to show my gratitude."

Little Pete was furiously grinding his teeth but Charlie talked on, confident now of success.

"I have observed the sad state of the resident Chinese. Many are sick and diseased, and all are poor. While I was walking the streets I made the acquaintance of a young missionary lady, a Miss Lorna Bascomb, who is doing good works to relieve their oppressed state. I understand that at one time she and her uncle, a Reverend Matthew Hewitt, ran a small mission in Brooklyn Alley. But they lost that" — he glanced meaningfully at Little Pete — "through an unfortunate circumstance. Therefore, gentlemen, I propose to donate seven thousand dollars" — he pushed the stack of bills and gold coins to the center of the table — "seven thousand dollars as a gift, Mr. Deputy Mayor, to the city of San Francisco to establish a new mission in Little China, dedicated to the relief of the Chinese people. The funding should be sufficient to establish a proper mission, with a small hospital in conjunction, a mission capable of feeding and clothing the indigent and relieving their suffering.

And, of course, Miss Bascomb is the only person to administer such a facility."

They were goggle-eyed at his generosity. "By God, sir!" Banker Roland cried, "this is an unparalleled gesture, unparalleled in the annals of San Francisco!" Deputy Mayor Backus clapped Charlie on the shoulder. "I accept, sir — for the city!" Captain Post swore fluently. "Beats anything I ever heard of!" Editor Neville said, "What a story this will make for the *Call*! I'll have it written up straight off!" He rubbed his chin, thinking, and spoke in headlines. "Magnificent offer by Colonel Charles Chaney!" Only Little Pete was silent. He seemed to have been poleaxed; his eyes were glazed. Finally, in a small squeak, he muttered, "All — those — money! How it happen me?"

Captain Post nudged Little Pete. "We're all going to do our part to make the new mission a success, Pete! Even if they are only Chinese, they deserve a fair shake! How about cleaning up that stinking Palace Hotel?"

"Right!" the deputy mayor said, "it gives the city a bad name!"

"As a banker," Mr. Roland said, "I must say that the Palace Hotel runs down the value of nearby properties. It's only good business to clean it up!"

"All — those — money!" Little Pete murmured, wiping a sleeve across his ashen face.

"As a gesture of goodwill, Pete," Charlie suggested, "you might very well consider donating that vacant lot on Sacramento Street to the mission."

Little Pete let out a howl. "Give to Christian mission — me — *give?*"

"You're damned right," the deputy mayor snapped. "Pete, your reputation in the city is none too good! So far we've kept the police off your neck, but I don't know how long we can keep it up. I'd suggest the gift of that property would enable us to protect you for a while longer. San Francisco is changing, you know. The old ways are vanishing."

Little Pete looked from one set of hard eyes to another. Finally he waved a fat hand. "All right — I do. But —"

"Thank you, gentlemen." Little Pete's fangs had been drawn. How accuse a gentlemen of cheating when he had turned over all his winnings to charity? "I bid you good day," Charlie said. "Perhaps now it is good morning. At any rate, it has been a very pleasant evening."

They crowded around to shake his hand, shower praises on him, congratulate the state of Tennessee on furnishing the Union with such a splendid fellow. Shaking hands with the deputy mayor, Charlie suddenly let out a cry. "Ow!"

Startled, they stared at him, "Colonel? What's wrong?"

He bit his lip in pain. Something had happened to the holdout! Perhaps a spring had broken, one of the ivory rods fractured — he didn't know what. But with the vigorous pumping of his hand by Deputy Mayor Backus, something had come loose. His groin was being stabbed by what felt like the point of a cavalry saber.

"Ah — ah —" He swallowed hard, squirmed, but the broken rod or whatever it was only struck deeper. "An

236

old wound, gentlemen, suffered at Cold Harbor when I was with Fitz Lee's cavalry!"

They commiserated with him but that didn't help. He heard, or felt, other disastrous sounds, realizing that the whole mechanism was coming apart, wrenched into a different configuration by the strain of newly aligned elastic bands. In fact, he was pulled off-balance. Backing away from his admirers, trying to bring off a departing bow, he was forced into a crabwise scuttle.

"Good night, gentlemen," he muttered through clenched teeth. "Thank you all again."

Hunched over like a bad Richard III in Mr. Shakespeare's play, he bumbled his way out the door, through the narrow passageways and corridors, across moonlit courts. The *boo how doy* were everywhere, greeting Little Pete's friend with ceremonious bows. He only hoped that the King of the Tongs had not somehow passed word to chop Charlie Callaway's head off at the ankles with a cleaver. In the deserted street he stopped, started to take off his coat to free himself from the torture of the broken holdout. But late passersby, drunk on rice wine, paused to stare at him. Cursing under his breath he hurried on. Not until he reached the rented room where Dan Pah Tsin and Loi San waited did he dare to rip off his coat. With their compassionate help he freed himself of the murderous contrivance.

San Francisco never saw Colonel Charles Chaney again. It was supposed that he had departed as modestly as he had come and was at home in

Chattanooga, Tennessee, doing good works among the newly freed Negroes.

"A great man," Deputy Mayor Backus later told a civic gathering at the groundbreaking on Sacramento Street for the new Christian Mission to the Chinese. "A real Southern gentleman!"

CHAPTER
THIRTEEN

Lorna, reading the *Call*, was first astonished, then incredulous, and finally tearful.

"A — a real mission, finally! Oh, Charlie, it's too good to be true! After all these hard times —"

"It's true, all right, Lorna." He clasped her in his arms but she pulled away, eyes brimming with tears.

"I still don't understand!"

"You don't have to understand, Lorna! It's come true. It's all over! I fought Little Pete and won!"

Dah Pah Tsin and Loi San sat in a corner of the dingy room in the Palace Hotel where Lorna had been ministering to a frail old Chinese dying of consumption. Their faces were inscrutable.

"But this headline mentions a Colonel Charles Chaney!"

He preened himself modestly. "That was me! Remember, my girl? Charles Chaney Callaway?"

Her voice was suddenly doubtful. "Charlie, this didn't come about because — because —"

"Because of what, my dear?"

"You weren't — gambling?"

Charlie's tongue stuck to the roof of his mouth. Finally he blurted, "Gambling? Me?"

"Because if this is the result of gambling, the whole thing is tainted! I know Uncle Matthew would turn over in his grave if —"

"Why, of course not, Lorna!" It hadn't been gambling, he told himself; it had been a sure thing! After all, when the chips were down, he had not even been able to *use* the holdout! He had bested the villainous Little Pete with superior skill, that was all. To the Old Gentleman he muttered, "Will that do? It really isn't a lie, if you look at it that way. Anyway, it was for a good cause! And I'll never gamble again! After Lorna and I are married, we'll —"

"Charlie?"

"Yes, dear."

"Whatever happened, I'm grateful to you for the part you played in it. Uncle Matthew would be proud of you, although in his early letters to me in Washington he had doubts."

"Yes, Lorna."

"But most of all, of course, I must thank Lord Jesus, who intervened somewhere along the way."

Charlie did not remember seeing Lord Jesus, but Lorna was probably right; the Old Gentleman might have put in a word with Jesus in Charlie's behalf. "Thank you, Lord Jesus," he murmured, and did not realize he had spoken aloud.

"Why, Charlie! That is very nice, to thank our Lord and Savior! I believe you *have* reformed!"

"Oh, I have — I have! And because I am now a different man, Lorna, there is something we must talk about."

240

"And what is that?"

"Our approaching marriage!"

"Our marriage?"

"Yes, Lorna dear! If you only knew how, in all my adventures — and misadventures — since I left the nation's capital, you have been the centerpiece of my thoughts! How often, a poor refugee sought by villainous men, I slept in rags, hungry and discouraged, sustained only by the memory of your sweet face!"

"Charlie —"

"How often I —"

"Charlie! Stop talking for a minute, please!"

Mouth still open, he stopped.

"I can't marry you!"

"Ah — what was that, my dear?"

"I can't possibly marry you, Charlie! I know you have become a different man — it is very apparent. And I am eternally grateful to you for what you have done to establish a new and better Christian Mission to the Chinese! But I am dedicated to improving the lot of these poor people! The gift of a new mission is a sign to me, a sign that my poor efforts have been blessed by Jesus! And in this great work, Charlie, there can be no room for the earthly diversion of marriage! I am in love with Jesus, Charlie." Demure, she turned her dark eyes modestly downward. "I intend to devote the rest of my life to him and his works."

"Ah —" Charlie swallowed hard and made stricken sounds. "Ah — ah —"

Lorna raised lovely dark eyes. She had never seemed to him so beautiful, so desirable.

"You *do* understand, don't you, Charlie? I will always remember you as a friend and benefactor!"

He felt as if he had been hit on the head with a bungstarter of considerable heft. Finally discovering his voice, he croaked, "I guess I do, Lorna! It was just — just that for so long I had hoped to — to —"

She kissed him, lips cool on the fevered brow. "You are my good old Charlie, and I will always be grateful to you!" Then she turned back to the elderly Chinese. Loi San brought her a basin and water; gently Lorna sponged the man's waxen cheeks. Over her shoulder she continued talking to Charlie but he did not hear. Unsteadily he made his way out into the squalor of the Palace Hotel and sat down on an empty bamboo crate. Dah Pah Tsin followed, squatted beside him, supporting herself with the tattered umbrella.

"I don't feel well," he confessed.

She grinned, a new cracking of the seams and fissures. "You not die, Misser Callaway!"

"I'm not so sure."

"You remember? I tell you — maybe? Maybe?"

I'm going to marry Lorna! We'll live in a big house on a hill and have lots of children and I'm never going to gamble again! Well, he had been a fool — and not for the first time in his life!

"Yes," he said bitterly. "I remember you tell me! Maybe, you said. Maybe!" Slowly he rose, put his arm around Dah Pah Tsin. "Thanks for all you did." When she turned up the wrinkled face, he kissed the leathery brow.

242

"You go," she muttered. "Find other woman, maybe. Be happy!"

He nodded. "I'll try." Disconsolate, he wandered off into the byways of Little China. It started to rain.

A schooner in the South Seas trade was anchored in the rain at the Pacific Street landing. On deck, a crew of brown seamen in singlets and sandals worked on a balky donkey engine. Steam hissed, the engine clattered, then fell silent. Charlie, wet and miserable, watched them with hands in pockets; gloom pervaded his soul. "That was not a good thing you did to me," he told the Old Gentleman. "And after I worked so hard, and reformed, too!"

The horny-fisted mate loosed a volley of curses and kicked the engine. "Damn stubborn invention of hell! Steam is the ruination of good sailor men!" As he spoke, a slanting ray of sunshine broke through the leaden clouds and illumined the little group; they stood like a tableau in a museum, limned in gold, caught for a moment in what looked to Charlie almost like a painting by Rembrandt — except, of course, for the steam engine. Was that a sign?

"I give up!" the mate shouted. "Heave the damned thing over the side!"

Charlie felt the Steamboat cards bulking large in his pocket. I'm never going to gamble again. Still, the Old Gentleman owed him something for the debacle. Maybe — just maybe — this *was* a sign. Maybe this was the course the Old Gentleman had chosen for him.

"I don't know whether I should trust you or not, but what the hell!" he murmured. "Ahoy the *Pacific Belle!*" he shouted.

They paused, the cursed engine balanced on the taffrail. "What do you want?" the mate bawled.

"I can fix that engine!"

"Go to hell!"

Charlie clambered up the ladder. "I can fix that engine!" He laid a knowing hand on the wet cast-iron cylinder. "Probably the valves are not adjusted right."

"Belay that!" the mate barked to the native hands. "Bring her down on deck so's we can see what this galoot can do!"

When the engine was steaming merrily along, pulley raising the mainsail aloft, Charlie wiped grease from his hands and stepped back. "There — that'll do her!"

"You're a marvel, mister," the mate admitted.

"I'm a good mechanic," Charlie said. "I fix teeth, too. Honor graduate of Dr. Motherwell's College of Dentistry and Animal Husbandry! Do you need a hand?"

The mate rubbed a bristled chin. "Three rascals jumped ship when we tied up here. You got papers?"

"Lost' em when the old *John B. Stokes* sank at her moorings," Charlie lied. "Been looking for a berth ever since."

"You'll do," the mate nodded. "We're getting under way for the Sandwich Islands. I'll straighten it out with the old man. Now give the men a hand with the lines!"

A growing sun split the clouds wide. The billowing sails of the *Pacific Belle* caught the wind and the

244

schooner began to move through the water. A few dockhands watched her go. One waved; Charlie waved back. Maybe this was where his fortune *really* lay, out there in the Sandwich Islands, where the sea was warm and palm-skirted maidens beckoned. Turning to the rest of the crew, he asked, "Any of you gentlemen ever try your luck at three-card monte?"